Dear Summer

by
K. Elliott

Editor: Audra Barrett, Barrett Books

audrab@usa.net

A love letter to Mama.

I am very proud of the space we are in now, for I have to admit, at one time I didn't think it would be possible.

Dealing with our imperfections, especially my own, this time didn't come easy. I wanted to put this out here because life is never promised, but it is often compromised, and so many times I have seen you compromise for me and my brother and sisters. There have been times that I didn't think anyone in the world cared a damn thing about me. Times when I sat in a jail cell thinking, what the hell have I gotten myself into. Nobody to write, nobody to call""but you were there for me. You would compromise your last but never your love.

As I reflect, now a grown-assed man, I want to say I appreciate everything you have ever done for me. The old saying is, you can't pick your family but you can pick your friends. If I had it to do all over again and I could choose, I would pick you. As a child I would often think, why couldn't I have been born rich? This is exactly how it was supposed to be. God is perfect; He makes no mistakes and we are exactly how we are supposed to be.

Thoughout the years I have struggled with issues of guilt and shame. We all have issues, but it truly takes a big person to admit"¦I was ashamed for being a have not, and I know this in turn sometimes made you ashamed because you provided me with everything you possibly could. Now I know this, and I am so apologetic for every bit of grief I caused you. I am sorry for putting others before family""people who really didn't have my best interest. Life is a lesson, and some people never get it. I have been fortunate to have your wise words to guide me. I know sometimes I can be a bit much and I may act like I have all the answers but I don't; and sometimes it is the simple things, like your wisdom, that has guided me.

I was not blessed with the ability to rap or sing, so I can't tell you this in a song. But I want you to know that I love you, Ma.

Acknowlegments

Industry peeps. Nakea Murray thanks for your friendship and insight. Shawna Grundy and Deja King, you have proven to be two of my best friends in the business. Thomas Long, my man 50 grand""my boy for life; turn that player card over nigga"¦you getting married. Naw, that's a blessing. I hope to find the right one, one day. Very jealous of that one dude. Jihad, holding it down in the A. My girl Jamise in the A. LaJill Hunt in VA. My nigga, Kwan holding me down in NY. Erick Gray, my nigga, keep doing your thing. Tushonda Whitaker repping Jersey. My girl Danielle Santiago, we're gonna hold Charlotte down. Shouts out to T.N. Baker, Treasure Blue, Blake Karrington keep doing your thing in the QC. Hallema down in the MIA. Mike Gainer in the MIA. All the book clubs, Coast to Coast Readers, Sisters on the Reading Edge in SanFran and all the other book clubs who have hosted me""I am grateful. Distributors, A&B, my man Kwame of Kwame Books, my man Hakim in Philly""thanks for the love.

Family. My dad, Walter Douglas. My cousin Big Boy, T Starr, Von, Sonya, Chris Star, Mellissa, Italian Mike, Sisters Crystal and Brandi, my brother E. Rico, we're gonna get u otta there nigga. Hawanni, Tammy, Missy, Linda, Regina, Jerry, my nieces and nephew. Milton, Twan. Pauline, Jacqueline and her crew. Angel, in B-More, Uncle Charles O, my cousin Bear in Minn. My new York Peeps. Wayne, Sherry, Donald, Barry, Aunt Gin. My cousin Rico hold it down. All my niggas on lock down hold your head. There are just too many friends and family to name, so if I forgot you I am sorry.

1

Tommy wanted to surprise her, but she wasn't home. He figured she had gone to the gym. Summer loved to workout, and she loved a surprise. That's how he knew she would like the surprise he would leave her""a red two-seater CLK. His boy Ditty couldn't believe Tommy was going to actually give her a car.

"Yo, this chick must have platinum pussy."

Tommy gazed at Ditty. "Mind your fuckin' business, nigga."

"I mean this ain't even your girl."

"Ditty, pull the car up to the end of the driveway and keep your thoughts to yourself."

"Okay. I think you're making a mistake. You can give that car to Angie. That's who you live with."

"Angie has a car. Just pull up to the edge of the house." Tommy lowered his voice. He didn't want to alarm the neighbors. Granite Falls was a peaceful subdivision with single-level homes and perfectly trimmed lawns. Ditty pulled the car almost to the tip of the house. Tommy hopped out of his smoke colored Range Rover with pen and paper in hand. He wrote Summer a letter. She loved letters. She loved to be romanced. Summer was from the South; a small town outside of Texas, and she was very much a lady.

Dear Summer,

I know I haven't seen you in a few days. I got your messages, and I've been wanting to call you back, but you know I've been grinding. Had to go to New York for a couple of days""you know, another business trip. I called your cell phone but didn't get an answer. I figured you must have been hitting the gym or something. I don't know what you're doing, but I do know that I miss you and I want to see you this week. I saw this bag in the city that I just knew you would like. It's a big bag and I know how you like those big bags, and it's made by Gucci, so I picked it up for you. I know you're also wondering what in the hell is this car doing in your driveway? I bought it for you. When I saw it I thought about you. I mean the color is red. The car is girly-girl like you, and it's a summer ride. I know you're going to look good in it. I can imagine you ripping down the ave with your hair blowing in the wind, wearing those big black sunglasses that I like. Let me know what you think, Summer. I miss you. And call me when you get home from the gym.

"Tommy, you're in this game too deep." Angie stared at him until he finally looked away. They'd had this conversation before and nothing seemed to be getting through to him. It seemed as if he was a deaf mute because he simply wasn't listening. She knew Tommy was a good man, a smart man, but he was going to jeopardize their future by selling these damn cars to those drug dealers. Ever since the day she met him, she'd envisioned a family with him""a life with him. She wanted his children, and she'd been vocal about it.

Angie was a tall lean woman with golden hair, golden skin, and hazel eyes. Tommy was in love with her, but he didn't like when she treated him like a kid, telling him what he should and should not be doing. He hated a nagging-ass woman. She wasn't like that when he had first met her. In fact, she was supportive of him and all of his ideas'""his legal ideas. Tommy met Angie one month after he'd gotten out of prison.

He faced Angie. "Baby, you act like I'm selling drugs or something."

"But the drug dealers are your customers. You do have something to worry about."

"What?"

Angie sighed and turned away from him. He grabbed her shoulder and she pushed his hand away. He looked surprised. He knew she was mad, and he didn't like it when she was mad.

"Baby, it's going to be okay. Trust me on this one. Nobody knows what I'm doing."

"Except dope dealers." She toyed with her hair, then turned and faced him. "Tommy, those fucking low lives are going to be your downfall."

"They're not going to tell. I'm doing them a service." He smiled. "Don't you see they need me?"

"Until it's you or them, Tommy. I can't believe you are not getting it. Why in the hell do you want to ruin everything? Don't you see we have a good life? We have a nice home and the bills are paid. Hell, your pops is a millionaire; we don't need anything else."

Tommy massaged his goatee. In deep thought, he knew she had a point. She always made good points, and that was the problem. She should have been a damn lawyer instead of a real estate agent.

"Tommy, I don't understand. Why do you like living on the edge?"

"It's the cash." He envisioned himself counting mountains of it. "It gives me a rush."

Angie sighed and threw her hands up in disgust; her breasts were about to burst out of her nightgown. "Tommy I give up."

He looked Angie in her face. She was sad; her eyes now watery and red. "Please don't give up on me."

"Give this shit up, Tommy, before it's too late."

"There is nothing to worry about."

"Tommy, have you forgotten your black ass just got out of jail? Have you forgotten how dirty your friends did you?"

"You don't know my friends, and shut the fuck up talking about my friends. They're dead and they can't defend themselves." Tommy was thinking about Twin and JoJo, his best friends since childhood, both of whom had been murdered.

A tear rolled down her face. She wanted to cry, but she held the rest of the tears in.

Tommy pulled her into his arms. Her breasts felt so good against his chest. Even while crying she was a beautiful woman. God he loved her.

"Tommy, I don't want you to lose focus on your life. You're too smart."

"My pop's money is his money. I have to make my own."

"Tommy, what about the family we'd planned to start? Have you forgotten about the family?"

Tommy grabbed Angie's hand and led her into the kitchen. He sat across from her at the kitchen table and stared. Her hazel eyes were hypnotic. "You don't understand, baby. What I'm doing I can never get caught."

"Nigga, you're a car thief. Do you think I want to have a life with a car thief?"

They both were silent. "Listen, Tommy, I'm sorry. It's just that"¦"

"Don't say it. I know you're concerned about me."

"Yeah."

"I've never had that before, really. I don't know if I can get used to that."

"Tommy, I want to be with you, not someone who sells cars to hoodlums."

"Hoodlums?"

"Yeah. Hoodlums."

She smiled politely. "I want a family."

"You know I want a family. I want you to give me a son, for my pops. You know he'll be so happy."

She looked at him but didn't say anything.

"I'm thirty-two now. I want a son."

"Tommy, you have to quit being a criminal."

"Who the fuck do you think you are, Miss high and mighty?"

She sucked her teeth. "You know what, Tommy? Why don't you just leave? Seriously. Pack your shit and leave."

Tommy stood and walked to the other side of the table. "Baby I just need a million dollars and I'm out of this business."

She looked up into his eyes. "Isn't that what you said before? This is the same shit you said before you got bagged and went to the feds."

"This is a different hustle, baby. This is more high tech."

"Tommy, you're a fucking car thief. What's high tech about thievery?"

"I don't steal cars. I buy cars and sell them."

"Yeah, but you buy from thieves."

Tommy said, "You're right. It's risky, and I don't want to go back to jail."

Angie stood up and sashayed across the room. Her walk was so seductive. She wore a tight gown that clung to her ass. Tommy watched. He knew that he had been blessed to find a woman like this; a real woman whom he could be honest with; a woman who knew his background. She was attracted to him because he had turned his life around.

"Tommy, you've come so far. You were doing so well. I mean, the anti-drug speaking engagements, the big brother mentorship"| Dream was so proud of you." Ms. Dream Nelson Smith had asked Tommy to do a seminar in a neighborhood center on the dangers of dealing drugs. She was an AIDS awareness advocate who had gotten caught up in the drug life before finding out that her boyfriend had infected her with HIV.

"I know," he said. His eyes shifted from her ass to her face.

"Tommy, I'm attracted to you because you're smart, not because of what you have."

"I know."

"So why don't you listen to me?" She ran her fingers through her hair. "You know your pops will be really disappointed if you go back to jail."

"Stop talking like that."

"It's a possibility."

"Hey, I'm gonna quit."

"Really? When?"

"I have three customers that need me and I'm done."

"You promise?"

He tried to kiss her lips but she pushed him away.

"Tommy, I need you to promise me."

"Yes, I promise." But Tommy had no intention of quitting. The money was coming too easily.

2

Q and Big Country sat on the hood of Q's 645 in the park watching some neighborhood niggas shoot hoops, when Q's brother Squirt walked up. "What's up Q and Country?"

"What's up with you, lil' nigga?"

"Tryin' to see you again."

"You finished already?" Q asked. He'd just given Squirt a brick of coke two days ago. He was surprised how fast Squirt was coming up in the game.

"Trying to be like you, nigga. I want the cars and the bitches."

"Be smart with your money because when it's over it's over and there's nothing nobody can do for you if you ain't got bread. You feel me?" Country asked.

Squirt dropped his head. "I feel ya, but I want a fat-ass ride, at least one, and I'm good."

Q smiled. "I can understand that."

A ball from the basketball court bounced off the rim and flew toward Country's head. He ducked and the ball hit Q's car.

Squirt picked the ball up and was about to toss it back toward a tall lanky kid who looked about fourteen, before Q said, "Give me that ball."

Squirt handed the ball over to Q who then walked toward the court. "Motherfuckas, if this ball hits my car again I'ma shoot this bitch."

A dark skinned kid named Eddie said, "Q, man, you know we ain't mean to hit your car. Man, come on, man, we playing ball."

Q slung the ball and it exploded into Eddie's face. Blood oozed from Eddie's nose before he fell to the ground.

"Q, that shit was uncalled for," one kid said.

"Who the fuck asked you anything?" Q said, as he grabbed the boy by the neck.

When Q let the kid go he pulled out his 9mm and blasted the ball. "Now, motherfucker, ain't nobody playing no motherfuckin' ball today, bitch-ass niggas."

Two boys picked up Eddie and walked him home.

Q walked back over to the car. "That nigga gonna tell his mama on you," Country teased.

"I hope not," Q chuckled.

"You afraid?" Squirt asked.

"Yeah. I'm afraid she ain't gonna give me no more of that good head."

"You fuckin' his mom?" Squirt asked.

Q laughed loud. "Yeah, so technically I'm like the nigga's daddy. You feel me?"

"Country said, "Nigga, you crazy."

"My word. I bought all the lil' nigga's school clothes and his shoes. That nigga wear a size fifteen."

"A fifteen?" Country asked.

"Yeah. They need to charge that motherfucker property taxes for his feet." Q laughed.

Squirt said, "Yeah back to business. I need one of those thangs, man."

"You got it. I mean, I got plenty," Q said.

"Cool. But seriously, I was thinking of getting me that new 745."

"How much money you got?"

"I don't know. I mean, I wasn't going to pay for it straight up in cash I was going to finance it""put it in my mama's name, you know. She's been working for twenty years."

"I can get you one for half price if you have the cash, nigga."

"How?" Squirt asked.

"Don't worry about it," Q said then pulled out his cell phone to call his boy Tommy. "Fatboy, come through. I'm at Tuckaseegee Park. Bring that piece with you."

"My nigga can get anything for half price."

"What the fuck. How the hell can he do that?" Squirt asked.

Q turned to Country. "Am I lying?"

"Naw, he can get anything. The nigga be having Porsche trucks, Benz wagons"\all kinds of shit."

"How?"

"They hot," Q said.

"Naw, nigga, I don't need them problems," Squirt said.

Q laughed then lit a Black and Mild cigar. "Nigga, don't be so fuckin' noid. I mean, all my shit hot. I don't even give a fuck. I own two Benz's and a Porsche, and I got my nigga looking out for the 600""I really want that 600."

"Why don't you just buy your shit legit? You have the money."

"I know I got the money, but it ain't even about the money, nigga." Q blew smoke from the cigar. "Didn't Country just tell you that we have to put back for a rainy day?"

"Yeah. I mean, I can dig it, but"""

"The paperwork is legit."

"Yeah?"

"How does he do it?"

"I don't know. I don't ask."

"All my cars are registered."

"To you?"

"Hell no." Q laughed then coughed. "No, I didn't say I was crazy, nigga. I still don't want anything to be in my name."

Tommy pulled up in a Mercedes Benz 500""dark blue with a smoke-gray tint.

"Yo, that shit is fire," Squirt said.

Tommy bounced from the car, shook Q's hand then Country's."

Q turned and put his cigar out. "Hey, Tommy, this is my nigga Squirt."

Tommy gave Squirt a pound.

"Q tells me you can have me riding."

"What ya looking for and how much you willing to spend?"

"BMW""the 745."

"I can get you one. It'll probably take a couple of weeks. How much you got to spend?"

Q said, "Cut my nigga some slack. He's one of my soldiers, you know."

Tommy laughed. "This is a $80,000 whip. I can probably give it to you with the paperwork and everything for forty large."

"Thirty-five," Q said.

Tommy saw the flat basketball with blood splattered on it a few feet away. He walked over to it and picked it up. "What the fuck happened?"

"My nine is what happened," Q said. "He pulled out his gun and grinned.

"Nigga, you shot the fuckin' basketball?"

"Yeah. Lil' niggas hit my car."

Tommy looked confused. "So, some kids hit your car with a basketball and you blasted the ball?"

"Not before he smashed one of the kid's face with the ball," Country said.

Q turned to Country. "That boy my son, I done told y'all."

Tommy shook his head. He couldn't believe it. "Come on, Q, man. You can't be making motherfuckers mad at you out here. I mean, you're a hustler. Niggas will tell on you just because."

"I know."

Tommy made eye contact with Q. "Do you really know?"

"Yeah, man."

"I hope so, because I don't want nothing to happen to you. I don't want you to go to jail."

"Why not?" Q asked.

"Because, nigga. I was there for four years and I didn't like that shit."

"So why you taking your chances with the cars?" Q asked.

"Because I like money. But you don't see me out her smashing lil' kids' faces in."

"Yeah, nigga. You be all up in the paper giving anti-drug speeches and shit."

Tommy smirked. "So you wanna take this car for a spin, Q?"

"But I want that 600."

"I can give you this 500."

"I want the 600. Really, I want the Maybach."

"And every fed in North Carolina will be after your black ass, nigga. You ain't Bill Gates."

"Motherfucker, you had one."

"And where did it lead me?"

Squirt asked. "The paperwork is official?"

"You will get a title that will match your VIN number. Don't worry about it. Everything will be official, trust me, you will get the title and everything."

"You mind if I sit in your car?" Squirt asked.

Tommy handed him the keys. Squirt sat in the car. "Yo, nigga, this shit is like sitting in a space ship. What is this again?"

"CLS 550."

"What you want for this?"

"Give me thirty and it's yours. It's a $70,000 car."

Squirt bounced from the car and handed Tommy the keys. "My heart is set on the 745."

"Give me 2""3 weeks and I will have it for you."

Squirt smiled. "I can't wait. They gone be hating on me."

Summer was tall and lean like a Victoria Secret's catalog model. Her legs seemed to go on forever, especially with heels on. But her most impressive feature was her smile. When she opened the door for Tommy, she was wearing only a skimpy G-string. She smiled and grabbed him by the shirt and led him to her living room, which was dimly illuminated with a red light. She took his belt off and handed it to him. "Spank me, Daddy."

"Are you serious?" Tommy said, not sure of what to make of her request.

She smiled then ran her tongue over her lip. "Of course I am, nigga. You know anytime you touch this ass I get excited."

Tommy's dick rose. It always worked with her. He'd had erection problems with some women, but Summer was too damned sexy. She had become addictive, but the best part about her was that she knew all about his woman and she didn't seem to mind. She just wanted to have fun and chill, and Tommy could respect that.

She pushed him to the sofa, slid her hand underneath his shirt and then frowned. "Tommy, I told you to get rid of those chest hairs. I don't like hair."

"I know, baby. I'm sorry."

She straddled his lap and kissed his neck. Her mouth was warm and he liked it. She whispered, "Tommy, grip my ass."

He put his hands on her ass and massaged her buns. Damn. She was so freaky.

"Uh"¦uh, she moaned, and then lay across his lap. All he could see was her ass cheeks and what seemed like a piece of thread traveling the crack of them.

"Spank me, Daddy. Spank me."

Tommy thought about Angie; thought about how much he loved her, but damn, he craved this feeling. He was obsessed over it. He cupped her ass and made it jiggle just a little; her ass was toned. Her whole body was. Unlike him, Summer worked out and she modeled part-time. She had even modeled for a fetish catalog. In her closet were all kinds of leather and lace, feathers, wigs, paddles, floggers, and handcuffs.

"Spank me, Tommy. Slap my ass and then rub it till it feels good."

Tommy opened his hand, held it in the air, and then slapped her ass.

"Tommy, harder."

He slapped her butt cheeks again.

"Now massage it. Make it feel good."

Tommy gripped her ass again and massaged it. Then he

slapped it. Summer moaned and gripped Tommy's pant legs.

"Tommy, that shit feels so good, baby.

Smack"¦Smack"¦Smack

"Yeah, Tommy. Yeah, baby." She gritted her teeth and held him tighter. She then stood up. Her ass looked wonderful.

She got on his lap. He gripped her ass and she pushed her tongue into his ear then whispered. "Tommy, my pussy is so wet, nigga. I want you so fucking much."

She moved her hand to his pants, unbuttoned them, and massaged his balls.

"I want your dick in my mouth."

He kicked his shoes off and she helped him take his pants off, and then pulled his boxers down. Summer dropped to her knees. When Tommy entered her mouth, his manhood swelled. She spit on his dick and licked it off. Damn. This bitch never ceases to amaze me, Tommy thought. Last week it was sex in the park, and the week before that she swallowed him""something he'd never experienced. He wondered what she would do today. She licked his balls before putting them in her mouth and began to suck. Tommy's head fell back and he felt like a king. She continued to suck and pull on his balls gently, and every few seconds she'd stop and look at him and say, "Tommy please cum in my mouth."

He tried to concentrate as hard as he could. He looked at those long, lean legs, her high heels and her beautiful face. He wanted to cum so badly but he couldn't. She scooted between his legs and continued to please him orally. Tommy pulled the string further up the crack of her ass. Summer moaned.

"Yeah, Tommy. Yes, Tommy. Smack my ass. Smack my ass until I cum."

Was she just saying this or could she really cum from somebody smacking her ass? Could anyone cum from this kind of stimulation? Tommy wondered, but he knew she got off on this kind of shit. When he slapped her ass, she took him deeper. His balls smacked her chin.

The red light made her body look golden and shiny and he could smell her. Some watermelon scent was now on him, and he loved it. He slapped her ass again and again. Summer began to tremble violently and her legs jerked but she kept sucking his dick. Tommy slapped her ass one more time and she came. Seconds later he exploded in her mouth.

3

Summer and Tommy lay in her bed wrapped in silk sheets. He stared at the wooden leaf-styled ceiling fan and wondered how his life had gotten so complicated in the last six months. Not only had he gone back to criminal activity, he was in love with two women. How in the hell have I gotten myself into this situation? He wanted to marry Angie, and he knew she was good for him""a strong, educated, upper middle-class black woman who would stand by him if he were doing the right thing. They had great times together. She taught him so much""helped him with his bad eating habits and taught him all about credit, something he knew nothing about. Before he had gotten arrested, he paid for everything in cash.

She had great family values. Her parents had been together for twenty-five years and that is what she wanted too. He knew because she'd expressed this to him more than once. And his father J.C. loved her and had expressed that he wanted her as a daughter-in-law. Tommy had to admit to himself that he was afraid of this kind of commitment, but he knew it was time. He was thirty-two years old. He wasn't going to get any younger and he wanted kids.

Summer sat up on the bed and stared at Tommy. When they made eye contact, she smiled and his heartbeat sped up.

"Tommy? What's wrong, Tommy? You look worried."

"Just thinking."

Summer took a deep breath. "Please don't tell me you're feeling guilty again."

"Kind of."

"Please spare me the details."

"I know this ain't right, but that ain't what I'm thinking about."

She stood and walked seductively to the bathroom. The door was open so Tommy yelled. "Why did you leave!"

"Because I don't want to hear about that bitch."

"You know I wasn't going to say nothing about her."

Summer reappeared wearing gray sweat shorts. She had put a do-rag on her hair.

"Summer, I want you too."

"Tommy, don't say shit like that. I ain't got no time for no bullshit."

Tommy put his hands behind his head and looked Summer straight in her eyes. "No bullshit. I'm too old for games."

"And, nigga, I'm too old for games. That's why when I met you, I wanted to just fuck and that's it."

"I know."

"Well, what the hell happened, Tommy?"

He pulled the covers up to his neck. He looked like a little chubby kid.

"Tommy, I didn't ask for this shit. I didn't ask for you to be getting no feelings, nigga."

"Why you so upset?"

"Because you say that you're in love with me."

"What's wrong with that?"

"Nothing's wrong with that, but you're in love with that other bitch, too."

Tommy didn't say anything. He pulled the covers past his head.

Summer walked over and yanked the sheets off him. "Tommy, look at me."

They made eye contact.

"Tell me you don't love her."

"I can't say that."

"That's exactly what I'm talking about. You can't say you don't love her. This shit cannot work."

"What do you mean?"

"Nothing, Tommy. Nothing. You'll never understand."

Scooter's hustle wasn't drugs; it was Nikes, counterfeit Nikes. He'd made a fortune off them, importing them from China for twenty bucks and reselling them for thirty-five. On any given week, Scooter could profit between thirty-five and forty hundred dollars. He and Tommy had met in the feds and had become cool. Because they were from the same city, they hung out and worked out together. Scooter had done ten years for drug conspiracy. The U.S. attorney had convicted him on pure hearsay, and when Scooter got out he swore to himself that he'd never sell drugs again. But he knew he'd hustle again.

Tommy drove up in the vehicle""it was a black Porsche Cayenne. Scooter was showing a nigga a BAPE hoodie when he looked up and saw Tommy. He turned and faced him.

"What's good, my nigga?"

Tommy smiled. Scooter was funny to him. He was always hustling, even in prison. He could have ten grand on his books but still be wheeling and dealing. Card games, dice games, loan sharking"you name it, Scooter was into it. He told Tommy that in the ten years he had been locked up, he made more than seventy-five grand.

The kid slid into the hoodie""perfect fit""then handed Scooter a fifty-dollar bill before walking away. Scooter said, "Don't fuckin' call me again unless you're trying to buy wholesale."

"Wholesale?" the kid asked.

"Twelve hoodies or more. Don't call me for a fuckin' fifty-dollar sale."

"How much will you sell them wholesale for?"

"Forty dollars each."

"Cool," the kid said, then hopped into a black Dodge Charger with twenty-inch rims, and scurried off.

Scooter hopped into his Denali and Tommy got in on the passenger side. Scooter gave him a pound. "Nigga, what's good?" Tommy said.

"Nothing, man. Still tryin' a make a dollar." He tossed the fifty-dollar bill under the armrest. Tommy noticed several bundles of money under the armrest. He figured it was maybe five or ten thousand.

"I see you doing good for yourself," Tommy said.

Scooter smiled. "Did you really think I would be doing bad?"

"No, not really, but I came to let you check out this Porsche truck I got. I remember you saying you wanted one."

"Not that one."

Tommy looked confused. "Why not this one?"

"This ain't the new one and the other one is a V8."

"I can give you this for thirty-five grand, Scooter. This shit has leather interior and a Bose sound system."

Scooter laughed. "First of all, I've never seen one that didn't come with leather interior, and that sound system shit don't impress me."

"Come on, Scooter. Man, thirty-five grand, you ain't gonna to find that nowhere."

"Tommy, come on, man. Nothing personal, it's just business. I like what I like, but if you can find me a Cadillac Escalade we can do business. I don't care what color it is."

"I got ya." Tommy opened the passenger door and, before he could get out, Scooter grabbed his arm and made eye contact with him. "Tommy, man, please be careful out there."

"I got ya, man. Don't worry about me; I ain't gonna do nothing stupid."

"I know, but your associations can get you in trouble, man. You know where we just came from."

Tommy smiled, gave Scooter a pound then got back into the truck and pulled off.

The white boys had called and said they had three Porsche 911s and a Yukon Denali. Tommy knew the Porsche would sell fast, but the problem was that he had two vehicles that had not sold, and he didn't want to have too much inventory and not enough money. Tommy had two hot cars that, it seemed, nobody wanted. He was sure he would have sold that Porsche Cayenne to Scooter. The car business was frustrating at times. Tommy thought, Niggas think I'm Car Max, trying to put in orders for specific make and models. That shit was annoying. Everybody he dealt with knew the cars were stolen and they would have to take what he could get. He could only tell his supplier what to look for. Sometimes the supplier could get it; sometimes they couldn't. He drove home thinking that he might have to sell one of the cars at maybe five thousand dollars above cost just to get his money out of it. He didn't want to, but he would have to sweeten the deal to get money for other inventory.

His phone rang. The caller ID read Summer. He didn't want to answer it, not because he didn't want to talk to her, but because he was almost home and he would have to get off the phone abruptly.

"Hello."

"Hey, baby. I was thinking about what we'd talked about."

"What did we talk about?"

"About you being in love with me."

"And?"

"Tommy, I don't like when you talk like that."

"Like what?"

"I'm talking about you talking like you really into me."

Tommy pulled his car into a nearby gas station. He knew that if he drove into his driveway he couldn't sit and talk. Angie would want to know what was going on and come out to be nosy.

"I don't like when you say you love me and don't mean it."

"I meant what I said."

"Tommy, I'm not the girlfriend type, and I damned sure ain't the wife type."

"I didn't say I wanted to marry you. You know I live with some-body."

Summer sighed. "I know you do, but Tommy, for the first time in my life it felt good that someone was into me."

Tommy laughed. "Come on. You're kidding, right? You're a fine-ass woman. I know you've had guys come on to you."

"Yeah, but they only want ass."

Tommy wished he hadn't shared his feelings with her, but after good sex he'd been known to blurt out some things that he'd regret later. He knew he truly had feelings for her, as he did Angie. "Can we talk about this tomorrow?"

"Tommy, I want to talk about it now. Why do we have to talk tomorrow?"

"Because, I'd just rather talk tomorrow."

"You've got to go home. Right?"

"You know that."

"That's why it won't work."

"What won't work?"

"Me and you."

"Why not? What's changed?"

"Tommy we've shared feelings about each other. That's what's changed.

He was getting frustrated. He hit the speakerphone button and placed the phone between his legs.

"I want to be with you."

"I see now."

"That's why I told you don't say shit if you don't mean it."

"I meant what I said."

"Okay, get rid of your girlfriend."

"I can't. It's just not that simple," Tommy said. He was afraid. He had never heard Summer sound like this before. She sounded so desperate for love.

"So, I have to play number two?"

"What the hell are you talking about?"

"I have to be the other woman."

"Summer, you knew I had a woman."

"Tommy, don't ever tell a woman you love her unless you're ready to be with her."

"I don't understand," Tommy said.

"I know. There is a lot you don't know about women. Goodbye."

4

Summer's friend Tonya had a dark-brown complexion, long flowing hair, and was a size four. She tagged herself on various relationship sites as the Black Barbie. She was very much a gold digger who had dated all types of men, from drug dealers to high-powered bank execs. Money was the only thing that mattered to Tonya. She and Summer sat in the waiting area of the nail salon.

"What do you think, chica"¦red or burgundy?"

"What are you talking about?"

"My nails, crazy. What are you thinking about?"

"Nothing."

"Come on, chica, I know you."

Summer thought hard about sharing her newfound feelings about Tommy with Tonya. She had known her for a while and Tonya had never given her a reason to think she'd ridicule her.

"Come on, baby. You can tell me. I mean, nobody knows you here anyway."

"It's about Tommy."

"What about him?"

"I think I like him now."

"Thank God. You need a man." Tonya smiled.

"Yeah, but it ain't that easy. I mean, Tommy has some issues."

"What's the problem? He looks okay and I've seen his Range Rover and the Benz." Tonya picked up a Marie Claire magazine. "So, I know he has money. By the way, what does he do?"

"I don't know what he does."

Tonya's eyebrows rose. "What do you mean you don't know? He just bought you that new Benz and you don't know what he does?"

"I've never asked him." Summer felt stupid for not knowing. She'd been seeing him for six months and never asked; not because she didn't want to know, but because she didn't want to seem nosy. She figured he was some kind of hustler or else he would have told her. She'd been with guys like him back in Houston. They were the types that you had fun with. They were cool because they would always have money and they took her and her friends out to eat. Nobody knew what they did for sure, but she knew that type rarely had a job. It didn't matter to her as long as they were fun""and Tommy was fun.

"He's never told you?"

"No, why?"

"He's hustling. Just be careful."

"Thanks, Mama," Summer said sarcastically.

"Just trying to protect you."

"Yeah. Just like you protected yourself when you were dating JJ. Adamant against hustlers until he bought you that diamond bracelet for your birthday."

"That's beside the point. I'm not with him."

"Not because he's a hustler, but because he decided to get married."

Tonya playfully stuck out her tongue. "It doesn't matter why I'm not with him."

Summer's face became serious. "Tonya, I want to be with this man."

"Why don't you get with him? It's obvious he likes you."

"Yeah, but he has a woman."

"Are they married?"

"No."

Tonya sucked her teeth and rolled her neck. "Hell, he ain't got no woman then."

"He lives with her."

"What?"

Summer felt dumb again. She avoided Tonya's eyes, stared into space and thought about her dilemma.

"How does he feel about you?"

Summer picked up an issue of Vogue. Beyonce was on the cover wearing a fitted yellow dress. Skimming through a few pages, she finally said, "He loves me too."

"The other bitch has to go then."

"It's her house."

"He needs to move into your house."

"What? We're not married."

"Come on, Summer. This is not the seventies. People move in with each other all the time. Get with the program."

"I don't know."

"I think Tommy's in the game," Tonya said adamantly.

"No. I don't think so."

"I think so. I mean, all the signs are there."

"But his pops is rich from the settlement with the State of North Carolina for false imprisonment. Remember the man that was with him that day we saw him at the gas station in the Yukon?"

"Yeah, I remember. His father had given me a business card. Said he had some rental properties."

Summer laughed remembering the day Tommy's father stared at Tonya's ass and came up with a lame excuse to give her his business card.

"What's so funny?"

"Just thinking about the day Tommy's father had given you his card. He know his old ass has to be at least twenty-five years older than you are."

Tonya looked away. "J.C. was kind of cool."

"What do you mean by that?"

"Just what I said."

"Girl, you did not fuck Tommy's father!"

Tonya didn't respond.

When Tommy's father opened the door, he looked worried. J.C., a usually well-groomed man, stood in the doorway with unkempt hair. He looked as if he hadn't shaved in a week. He let Tommy in and they walked to the kitchen. Tommy sat at the table and J.C. sat at a barstool near the kitchen counter. "Tommy I'm sorry I called you so early, but I had to talk to somebody and you're the only person that I have now, son."

"What's wrong?"

"Tommy, I'm broke."

"What the hell are you talking about Pops?" Tommy laughed. There was no way his father could be broke. The state had awarded him $3 million for false imprisonment four years ago. He had invested in real estate at the advice of one of his friends.

J.C. looked away for a moment then turned back and made direct eye contact with Tommy. "Yeah it's true. I've blown all the money, son."

"No way!"

"When I paid the taxes on the money I was down to 1.5 million, gave you $100,000, and I owed your attorney over $80,000 for representing you. I was left with a little over a million dollars."

"Okay, and you blew it?"

"Tommy, a million dollars is not a whole lot of money. Hell, you know better than anybody. You've had a million dollars before."

"Pops, I lost my money in the drug game; you don't sell drugs."

"I know."

Tommy stood from the table. "So what the fuck are we going to do now? I mean, you always telling me to keep my nose clean and don't get into any more shit, and you've done gone and blew the fuckin' money!"

"Son, don't talk to me like that."

Tommy looked at his father. He looked broken. J.C. looked as if he wanted to cry. Tommy walked toward the door without saying a word before J.C. called out to him, "Son."

"What the hell do you want with me?"

"Son, I'm about to lose my house."

"What the fuck? You're about to lose the house too?"

J.C. sniffled, holding back his tears. "Yeah son, and two of my other properties."

Tommy stared at his father for a long time. He wanted to pound him in the face. How in the hell could he be so damn stupid? How could he have fucked up that much money that fast without any bad habits? "Pops, you know what that means then."

"What?"

"I gotta do what I gotta do."

"Tommy please don't do nothing crazy."

"Everybody tells me this shit but nobody ever comes up with money to help me do a goddamned thing, but everybody always has their fuckin' hand out."

"Son, I'm sorry," J.C. said, then hugged Tommy.

Tommy pushed him away. There was no time for that mushy shit. He had to get busy. He had to sell cars and fast. "How much money do you need?"

"I need thirty grand, then next month I can refinance one of the houses, pull out $75,000 in equity, and hopefully sell the rest to get from under them."

Tommy turned the doorknob. "I will have the money for you in one week."

"Thank you, son."

5

Summer and Tonya were about to leave the nail salon when she received a message on her Blackberry from Tommy's phone. Summer read it then passed it to Tonya.

Dear Summer,
I thought about what you said"¦that I need to be with you. Just give me some time to sort things out. I mean, I just can't up and leave her like that, you know. She was there for me when I had just gotten out of prison, so it's not that easy to cut her off. I called your phone but you didn't answer. I don't know. Maybe you don't want to talk to me or something, but if you get this message, give me a call when you get a chance.
Tommy
Sent via Sprint PCS Blackberry

Tonya passed the phone back to Summer.
"He emails you?"
"Yeah."

"But he's a thug."

"Because he knows I like that. I don't really like talking on the phone, wasting my minutes. Shoot me a text or an email. I like emails. I like writing."

Tonya looked at her strangely. "It's the writer in me, also the girl. Nothing beats an old fashioned love letter."

"Don't tell me he writes you love letters, too."

"He has."

"You're weird."

"Not really. I just want to be romanced sometimes. What's wrong with that?"

"So, are you going to get with him?"

"I don't know, but I'm falling for him, and fast."

Tommy and Ditty met the white boys at a coffee house in South Charlotte; the four of them sat in the back corner of the cafe. The white boys were two computer geeks who had learned to break into cars by using laptops to breakdown the security systems; that was all Tommy knew. He'd met Matt in federal prison. Matt had done six months for a computer related crime. On the inside, since they were both from Charlotte and liked the Tar Heels, they'd become cool. Matt, who was a redhead and the older of the two white guys, spoke first. "We got you another 645. It's blue. You're gonna love it."

"I told you I need a 745."

"Yeah we know, but you're gonna love this one, I promise," Jay, the other white boy, said. He was a lanky kid, about twenty-three; he wore a Duke Blue Devils ball cap.

"What color is it?"

"Blue. I already told you that," Matt said.

Tommy became angry. "I know, motherfucker. Do you know how many variations of blue there are?"

"Can't really describe it," Matt said.

"It's kind of like that ultra blue. Trust me. You're gonna like it. If not, paint it another color."

Ditty grinned and nudged Tommy. "That ultra blue is fire."

"What else do you have?"

"A Grand Cherokee," Jay said.

Ditty looked disgusted. "Nobody we know is gonna want no shit like that."

"Well that's all for now. I'll have two more Porsches in two days; just getting the paperwork right, you know."

"Cool. I think I'll take the 645. What you want for it?"

"Twenty-five," Matt said. Then he turned to Jay, who pulled his ball cap farther down on his head and took a deep breath.

"Last time you gave me a 645 for twenty."

"Yeah. The last time it was an "'06, this one is an "'07 with 13,000 miles on it."

"I'll give you twenty now and five later."

Jay looked at Matt then back at Tommy. "I don't know if we can do that."

"Why not? I mean, I've spent over two hundred grand with y'all in the last two months. How in the hell are you gonna let $5,000 come between us?"

"Can't do it, Tommy. I got somebody willing to give me thirty for it, but I wanted you to see it first because I'd promised you a 745."

"Ain't this a bitch," Tommy said. He pulled his cell phone from his waist. Q answered on the second ring. "Yo."

"Q, got a 645, ultra blue, do you want it?"

"How much?"

"Forty stacks."

"I don't want it, but my brother might. But you know he really wanted the 745."

"Can't get it, but this one is hot""""'07, brand new; only 13,000 miles on it."

"Meet me at the barbershop at 7:00 tonight with it. I'm sure he'll take it."

"Okay." Tommy terminated the call. He smiled and then looked at the white boys. "Meet me here in two hours. I'll have the money for you." They all shook hands. Done deal.

Q and Squirt were parked in front of the barbershop in Q's Lexus truck when Tommy and Ditty pulled up in the new car.

Q and Squirt hopped out of the truck and approached Tommy, grinning. "I'll take it."

"This motherfucker is straight fire," Q said.

Tommy got out of the car, handed Q the keys and said, "I need forty-five for it."

"I'll give it to you," Squirt said. "I ain't gonna do shit with this one, no rims or nothing."

Q opened the door of the car, examined the interior and then turned to Tommy. "I need one of these too."

Tommy looked at Q like he was stupid. "Nigga, you already got enough cars. Don't make yourself more of a target than you already are."

Q stared at Tommy, looking serious. "I thought about what you said the other day and I'm looking for a way out of the game."

"Just stop, nigga."

"And do what? Steal cars?"

Tommy looked around, making sure nobody had heard Q. "Okay, motherfucker, let the whole world know what I do."

Q turned the ignition then looked at Tommy. "I'm sorry. Hey, me and Squirt are gonna go around the block. Okay?"

"Cool. Go ahead. I'll be waiting on you."

When they were out of sight, Ditty said, "I don't like that motherfucker Q."

"Q's okay. He's just a young nigga with a little bit of money that don't know how to act."

"Tommy, be careful with that nigga. I don't trust him," Ditty said.

"It's gonna be okay. I don't think he'll do anything to hurt me."

"The nigga is stupid and he probably has the feds already on his trail."

Tommy patted Ditty on his shoulder. "It's gonna be okay. Trust me."

Q and Squirt pulled up. Q opened the door of his truck and Squirt climbed out and produced a Nordstrom's shopping bag full of money.

Tommy looked at it and said, "How much is that?"

"Forty stacks."

"I need forty-five."

Squirt glanced at Q and then looked back at the sparkling BMW. "I thought you said forty."

"Yeah I did, but I got somebody wanting to pay forty-five."

"Come on, Tommy, man, you know. Is this how you gone treat family, man? You know that I give you all kinds of business."

Tommy laughed. He pointed to the car and placed his arms around Squirt's neck. "Nigga, just imagine the bitches you're gonna get with this machine."

Squirt smiled and turned to Q. "Loan me the five G's "~till I get home, man."

Q walked to his car, opened his glove compartment and reappeared with a bank envelope. He counted out fifty one-hundred dollar bills and passed them to Squirt, who gave Tommy the money.

Tommy counted the money then handed Squirt the keys. "The paperwork is in the glove compartment. You can go get it registered."

Squirt smiled, looked at Q, then Tommy and walked toward the car. He then looked back once more and said, "The bitches gonna love me, man."

6

Inside Summer's bedroom, Tommy stood over her face, holding his dick. He dropped his balls in her mouth. In and out. This was called tea-bagging and Summer loved when Tommy did this. She would make humming sounds that drove Tommy wild. He could tell she enjoyed it, too, because sometimes she'd cum. She hummed on his balls for five minutes before she stood up from the bed and walked to the opposite bedroom wall. She pressed her hands against the wall, turned to Tommy and said, "You know I like it from the back."

Tommy put his hands around Summer's waist and she lowered her ass. She always had to lower herself because she was an inch taller than him.

"I don't have a condom."

"I don't give a damn, Tommy. Just put it in."

He entered her. She moaned softly. "Oh baby, my pussy is so wet."

"Hell, yeah," Tommy said.

Tommy moved in and out and smacked her ass hard. He was enjoying watching the contrast of their skin. Tommy was chocolate, he was much darker than Summer. He looked at her hair, which was stringy but beautiful. It was still hard to believe he had someone like Summer in his life.

"Tommy, smack my ass."

He continued to hump. He removed his right hand from her waist and slapped her ass hard.

"Yeah, baby. Yeah."

"You like that?"

"You know I like that shit."

Tommy smacked her ass again.

"Pull my hair, nigga. Pull my hair."

He grabbed a few strands of her hair and pulled.

"No, nigga. Pull my hair."

With his right hand again, he grabbed a handful of Summer's tresses and pulled hard.

"Yeah, like that."

"Damn, baby. I like that freaky shit."

"This ass is all yours, Daddy."

Tommy's erection stiffened and his dick grew a little inside her. Summer threw her ass back toward him and smiled.

He released her hair and smacked her ass.

"That's my spot!"

"Whose pussy is this?"

"Baby don't move, please don't move."

Tommy yanked her hair and Summer began to go into convulsions, and when she came, he came seconds later.

Summer walked to the bathroom and cleaned herself up while Tommy lay on the bed. She threw him a towel and he cleaned off his testicle area and his penis.

"I'm a happy woman right now."

Tommy was happy he could now satisfy women. There was a time when he couldn't get an erection, but now, thanks to herbal medication, not only could he get hard, he could last for hours if he needed to.

Summer slid into a pair of blue running shorts that were lying beside the bed. She left her breasts exposed. She hopped into the bed with Tommy. He grinned at her.

"I love you, Tommy."

He stared into her eyes. He saw his reflection. He was still grinning. He didn't say anything though.

"Tommy did you hear me?"

"Yeah."

"You don't love me?"

"Yeah. Of course I love you."

"Why didn't you say something?"

"What do you want me to say?"

"I need you to say that you love me too, Tommy."

"You know I love you."

She shifted her body into his then put his arm around her. Tommy placed his hand on her ass. He liked the shape of it and the way it felt. He knew this turned her on and he wanted more sex. He could never get enough of her.

"Tommy can I ask you a question?"

"Yeah of course."

"When are you going to leave her?"

He released her and moved his other hand away from her ass and stared at the ceiling. He was still sweating. He stood on the bed, pulled the chain on the ceiling fan and watched the fan swirl around.

"Tommy, when are you going to leave her?"

"I don't know."

"Tommy, look at me," she demanded.

He met her eyes. He could tell she was now in love with him by the way she looked at him.

"Tommy, I want to be with you. I want to have your baby."

"Are you ready for kids?"

"Tommy, I'm ready. I'm twenty-eight, and I know you're a good man. I know you will be a great father."

He turned away from her; his back was now facing her. She put her arms around him and held him. "Tommy, I want you all to myself."

"I know. But what are we going to do? I mean, I am a car thief and you're"¦I don't know what you are."

"Tommy I will be okay. Soon as I write my book, I'ma be paid. I know this girl, Danielle Santiago. She goes to my salon. She got a six-figure book deal and she's livin' lovely."

Tommy turned and faced her. He pulled her close. His hands were now on her ass. The soft feeling of her ass made his dick stiffen.

"What's your book about?"

"A female madam."

"A madam?"

"Yeah. She runs a call girl service."

"This shit is inspired by who?"

Summer sucked her teeth, she knew that once people knew what her book was about they'd assume that the book was based on her life. "I don't know. It's kind of like Heidi Fleiss, but hood."

Tommy laughed. "But I know you must have some experience in this shit."

She looked annoyed but didn't say anything. She couldn't believe he was saying she must have been a whore. "Tommy I'm not going to say nothing to you."

"Why not?"

"What if I told you I'd been a whore? Would it matter?"

"No. Hell no, baby. I didn't mean it like that." He pulled her close.

"Good, because I'm not."

He was silent. He knew that he'd offended her. They held each other until he dozed off.

Dream Nelson introduced Tommy to the fourteen boys who'd been labeled at-risk by the school district. Standing in front of the small class, Tommy looked out at the boys. They all looked hopeless and like unwanted misfits. They looked familiar not because he knew them, but because they represented him. He was happy to speak to the boys, not because he was a role model; he was nobody's role model. Hell, he was a part of a large automobile theft ring. He was glad he could talk to them because nobody else would. It was sad that there were hundreds of African American doctors, dentists, attorneys, and other professionals, but most were unwilling to give their time. Though Tommy felt like a hypocrite for speaking to them, he hoped that at least one would hear his message. He secretly hoped he would listen to himself. His girlfriend Angie sat beside Dream as Tommy spoke about his time in prison. The boys all looked scared when Tommy told them how he was strip searched and shackled whenever he was taken outside of the prison.

A boy on the back row with a large egg-shaped head and chapped lips asked, "Were you ever raped?" Several people giggled.

Tommy even laughed before saying, "No. But I've heard of it happening." He was used to that question. He knew it would come up. It always did whenever he talked about his prison stay. Women would especially want to know if he'd been raped, and had he raped someone. They wanted all the details of his prison stay. Was he on the down low? He glanced at Angie.

She was dressed impeccably in a blue blazer and heels. Her hair was pulled back. She made eye contact and smiled. He could tell by her facial expression she was proud of him.

Tommy paced. He was a little nervous at his speaking engagements. When he had first started speaking he would often forget what he wanted to say. Now he had become better and he would bring a yellow legal pad with brief directions on where he wanted to go with his speech. A tall lanky kid with braids who was wearing a "Stop Snitching" T-shirt, stood up. "Hey, what did you go in for?"

"I was an ecstasy dealer."

"Did somebody snitch on you?"

Tommy giggled. "I guess you could say that."

"Don't you want to kill them?"

Tommy laughed out loud this time. Angie's lips tightened. Tommy could tell she was interested in his response. The truth of the matter was that he did want to kill the white bitch that set him up. But he couldn't say that. He stopped laughing and said, "Initially I did, but I realized that I was the problem, and I got what was coming to me."

"How much money did you make?"

"Enough," Tommy said. Though millions had gone through his hand, he couldn't make it seem as though he was advocating drug dealing.

Another kid asked, "Don't you miss the money?"

"No. I'm glad I got my freedom." He paced, and then referred back to his legal pad. "When you're on the inside, nobody cares about you. Nobody cares about how much money you made. Those people just want their time. If your mom dies, you may or may not be allowed to attend the funeral."

Dream stood and looked at her watch. "We have another speaker, Attorney William Farrow," she announced.

A couple of kids on the front row booed, and someone yelled, "I don't wanna see no damn attorney."

Dream gave Tommy a hug and he walked over and took a seat beside Angie.

7

A wedding picture sat on Dream's desk. It was hard for Tommy to believe that she was HIV positive by looking at her. She was stunning. Her skin was dark and flawless. Her teeth were the color of milk.

Dream's dress was fire-truck red and it gripped her ass wonderfully. Tommy looked at her in a way Angie wouldn't notice. He knew if she did notice him staring he'd simply play it off by saying she has HIV. Of course he didn't have interest in her because of that, and she was married. Dream took a position behind her desk and asked Tommy and Angie to take a seat.

"Tommy, I want to thank you for coming out today."

"I'm glad I came."

Angie raised her eyebrow. "Anytime you need him, he'll come. Ain't that right, Tommy?"

Dream stood and walked to a table that was behind her

desk. Tommy looked at her ass again, thinking Damn this bitch is beautiful. It's too bad she has HIV.

When she kneeled to get her briefcase, he saw her stockings and he got an erection.

She popped open the briefcase and handed Tommy a brochure. The brochure had a picture of a red-headed white man. The caption read, "This man made over 1 million dollars last year for speaking."

Tommy looked at it and looked back at Dream. "What's this?"

"Tommy, I want to help you get paid for speaking; for sharing your experience. I made over $100,000 last year with public speaking engagements."

"But who wants to hear my story?"

"That's what I thought, Tommy."

Tommy wanted to say, "But you have HIV."

Angie grabbed his hands. "Tommy, I think you will be great at this."

Dream smiled brightly. "I think you should give it a shot."

"Baby, it's legal money," Angie said.

Tommy took a deep breath and wondered to himself. Could he really live off a hundred grand a year?

Tommy and Ditty followed the waitress to a booth in the back of the Outback Steakhouse. When they were seated, they both ordered lemonade. When the waitress returned with the drinks, Ditty said, "How is life treating ya, lover boy?" Ditty grinned, revealing yellowish green teeth. Tommy looked at his friend's mouth. He had wanted to tell him several times that a visit to the dentist wouldn't be deadly. But he could never muster up the nerve to tell his friend that his breath stunk.

Tommy met his eyes. Ditty had a smirk on his face. He was being sarcastic.

"What the hell is that supposed to mean?"

"I mean just what I said. Are you still in love with two women?"

Tommy took a deep breath and said, "Yeah."

Ditty leaned forward and whispered. "You're going to need

to cut one of those bitches off if you want to be successful. Out here you got to be focused if you want money."

"Nigga, I'm your boss. What the fuck are you talking about? Did you forget I got your dope-dealing ass off the street and introduced you to a new hustle?"

Ditty sipped his lemonade and almost choked. "Yeah I remember, but all I'm saying is with bitches comes responsibility, and when you have responsibility you spend money." Ditty took another sip from the straw. There was no more lemonade in the cup, only ice. He shook the ice before pouring it into his mouth.

The waitress appeared. They both ordered the 12oz. Strip steak with baked potato.

Ditty looked at Tommy seriously. "Tommy, I don't think that Summer bitch is good for you."

"Nigga, you don't know her."

"I just don't like her vibe."

"You never like anybody."

"It's not that. I just realize the motherfucker's intentions."

"How can you say that about her? You've never met her."

"The bitch is beautiful"|I mean drop dead gorgeous. She's a gold digger."

"Nigga, I've always had beautiful bitches."

"You've always had gold diggers, too."

Tommy thought about what Ditty had said. He didn't particularly like what he was saying, but it wasn't the first time he'd heard that, and he knew if he didn't have money and cars that he probably wouldn't be with Summer.

"Angie ain't no gold digger," Tommy said.

"Yeah, and that's why you should be with her."

The waitress came and sat their plates down, then refilled Ditty's lemonade.

Tommy cut into his steak and added some A1. "Summer's a good person."

"I don't doubt it, but I just get a vibe about her."

Tommy knew that Ditty was loyal to him and wasn't just being malicious, but he couldn't let Summer go.

"Tommy, we got a good thing going. I'm just saying that you don't need distractions."

"You think she's a distraction?" He cut the steak into small pieces then bit into one.

"Yes. She's a distraction."

"She loves me."

"Did she tell you this?"

"Yeah."

"But you love Angie, right?"

"Yeah," he said, avoiding Ditty's eyes.

"But you like this bitch, too." Ditty said.

A frown appeared on Tommy's face.

Ditty drank the rest of his refill and said, "I'm sorry, Tommy."

8

Tommy was on the way home, driving fast. Angie had just called him to say dinner was ready. She had cooked his favorite""baked chicken and rice. He would stop at the convenience store around the corner from the house to buy himself a Coke. He knew he would have to hurry and drink it before he got home because Angie always chastised him about sugar products. It had been easy for him to give up soft drinks and candy in prison, but in the real world the pressures made him want to do something. Since he wasn't going to ever do drugs"¦his addiction was sugar. He figured it could be worse. At least he wasn't smoking crack. He stopped at the store, went to the case and got a can of Coke. Just as he was about to walk up to the counter, he noticed a special on the Mr. Goodbars""two for one. He would eat one now and the other tomorrow. Just as he was about to peel the wrapper off, his phone rang. The caller ID read that it was Q. "What up, Q?"

"Squirt went to jail today."

"What? You're lying," Tommy said. He climbed into his car and put the candy and the drink on the passenger seat.

"Yeah, he got caught with nine ounces."

"Soft or hard?" Tommy asked. He knew that in the drug business nine ounces of crack is a death sentence, but if it was coke, he would have another chance.

"I don't know. I haven't spoken to him yet."

"Damn. That's too bad."

"Yeah it really is."

"Hey, man, I will call you tomorrow. I have to go home to my lady."

"Tommy, that ain't all."

"What you talking about?"

"He got bagged in the car you sold him. The police is saying the car was stolen."

"What the fuck you mean they said the car was stolen? I've been stopped plenty of times and ain't nobody ever said shit to me."

"Tommy, they said the car was stolen. That's what Squirt's girl said."

"Nigga, all our cars are stolen, but the paperwork is legit."

"Hey, Tommy, I hope for your sake, nigga, the paperwork is legit."

"What the fuck is that supposed to mean, Q? Are you threatening me? Cuz I ain't nobody's punk, nigga."

"Fuck you, nigga." Q hung up the phone.

Ditty cracked open a vanilla dutch and poured the greenery into it. This would be his second blunt for tonight. He and Tommy sat at his kitchen table. "Nigga, get you another beer from the fridge," Ditty said.

Tommy walked over to the refrigerator and grabbed a Bud Light. He rarely smoked weed. Never had he bought it, but maybe once or twice a year he'd take a hit. He generally didn't like the way it made him feel, but he would drink beer, especially when he was depressed. He opened his beer and sat back at the table with Ditty.

"Yeah, that nigga Q said Squirt got bagged."

"With what?"

"Said he got caught with nine ounces of coke."

Ditty put the blunt up to his already burnt lips and inhaled. His eyes tightened, making him look like a very dark Asian. "Nigga, I don't give a fuck. That's his problem."

"I know, but Q is trying to blame the shit on me, saying the paperwork wasn't right."

Ditty offered Tommy the blunt, but he refused for the third time and Ditty puffed again before asking, "So, how you want to handle it?"

"What do you mean?"

"Do you want to go to war or what?"

"No, man. I want to find out what's going on."

Ditty disappeared to the back room and returned with a black golf bag.

Tommy laughed out loud. "Just cuz that weed done made you look part Asian don't make you Tiger Woods."

"Right. Where Tiger carry clubs in his bag, I carry tools." He opened the bag and pulled out an AK-47 and a Tech-9 and laid the bag on the floor. "I will blow Q's fuckin' block off. I never liked that nigga."

"I don't think it's gonna come down to that."

Ditty held his blunt in one hand and the Tech-9 in the other. He puffed his blunt one final time. "He better hope not, because I will blow the nigga's back out."

Matt was wearing an extra small Abercrombie & Fitch T-shirt and ripped jeans. He held some kind of techie magazine in his hand. He and Tommy took a seat in a booth at Starbucks. Tommy started by saying, "The paperwork was fucked up on the car."

"Impossible."

"What do you mean, impossible?"

Matt looked Tommy straight in his eyes. He didn't flinch and neither did Tommy. "You know, I've been doing this for two years, and it's just like I said'""impossible."

"My friend got busted with drugs in the car."

"Not my problem," Matt said nonchalantly and opened his magazine.

"He's saying the car was the reason he got pulled."

"Did he get charged with possession of a stolen vehicle?"

Tommy thought about it. Q never said Squirt had been charged with possession of a stolen vehicle. "I don't know."

"Find out."

Tommy called Q from his cell. He answered on the third ring, "What?"

"Did Squirt get charged with possession of a stolen vehicle?"

"I don't know."

"What's his last name? I will call downtown to see what's going on."

"Not giving you his last name." Q hung up the phone.

Tommy said, "I will find out if he got charged with possession of a stolen car."

Matt stood, folded the magazine and placed it in his pocket. "Tommy, somebody is shitting you, friend. The car wasn't the reason your friend got busted."

Tommy looked confused.

Matt put both hands in his pocket. "Tommy, we've never had this happen."

Tommy narrowed his eyes. "So, Matt, tell me" how does the operation work?"

Matt shifted his feet back and forth, and then his eyes met Tommy's. "Now, you know I can't tell you that."

"Why not?"

"Because I can't, man. Besides, the scheme is too sophisticated."

"Motherfucker, I spend at least $200,000 with you per month."

Matt shrugged his shoulders. "Sorry, Tommy, but I can't." He extended his hand.

Tommy frowned and left Matt's hand dangling. "Whatever, motherfucker."

9

Dear Summer,

I woke up this morning thinking about you. I haven't spoken with you in a couple of days and I called and left you a message. I was wondering if you and your girl would like to hang out with me and my boy Ditty. Some time today, let's go get some Japanese food or something. Call me when you get the message.

From Tommy
Sent via Sprint PCS Blackberry

After Summer read the message she immediately called Tommy. He picked up on the second ring. "Hey, baby. Didn't think you would be up."

"You know I get up early in the morning to write."

"Yeah, I know, but I guess that's what I thought you'd be doing."

"I can't seem to get myself going today."

"So you want to go to lunch?"

"Yeah. I'd like that. I will have to call Tonya though, to see if she wants to hang out."

"Tell me about her."

"Why you want to know about her?"

"My boy Ditty need a woman in his life."

"Is he like you?"

"What do you mean?"

"You got two women in your life," Summer said. She knew this would start an argument, but what the hell.

"I don't have two women in my life."

"Nigga, you know you got two women. Have you forgotten you living with a woman?"

"No. It's not going to always be like this. So do ya'll want to go to the restaurant or not?"

"What restaurant?"

"Kabuto's."

"I guess. I'll call Tonya," Summer said. She went into the bedroom. She pulled off her jeans and stood with her panties on. "Tommy, I want phone sex."

"I'm driving."

"Pull over. I got on that G-string that you like. You know, the one with the beads on it." She lied. The truth was she had on boy shorts but she wanted phone sex and she knew this would be the only way that he would participate.

"The pink ones?"

"Yes," she moaned.

"Baby, I can't pull over. I have somewhere to go."

Summer pulled her panties to the side and stroked her clitoris. "I'm stroking my clit."

"And I'm pulling over to the side of the road."

"I'm imagining your head between my legs," Summer continued. She could feel the moisture arising between her legs.

"You tasting my clit. You're licking up and down and the top of it. Did you pull over yet?"

"I'm in the Wal-Mart parking lot."

Summer moaned. "Tommy, your fingers are going in and out my pussy while you're tonguing my clit."

Tommy said, "I got my hand on my dick, stroking it."

"I turn over on my stomach and you start eating my pussy from the back."

"I want to put it in."

"Put it in, Daddy, put it in," she said. She kept stroking her clit until she brought herself to an orgasm. "Thank you, Daddy."

"What the hell"¦I know you didn't cum."

"Came hard, too. I'll get you on the next one."

"One o'clock at Kabuto's."

At an eloquent little restaurant downtown, Tommy and Ditty waited on Summer and Tonya. The girls arrived fifteen minutes later. Ditty was smiling hard as hell when he met Tonya. Her jeans were gripping her ass nicely and her skin was flawless. He wanted to fuck her. She extended her hand but he asked for a hug. She smiled and complied. He held her for a long time before she pushed him and said, "Would you ease up?" She frowned.

"Bitch, you ain't all that," Ditty said.

"Why I gotta be a bitch?" Tonya said.

Ditty turned to Tommy. "I'm leaving, man."

"No. Don't leave."

"Tommy, let the motherfucker leave. The nigga ain't my type anyway."

Summer grabbed Tonya by the arm. "Come on. Chill out."

Tonya frowned. "I don't like niggas like that. I mean, all because I wouldn't let him have his way with me, I'm a bitch."

A waitress appeared and led the four of them to a booth.

Tonya sat on the inside of Ditty. He extended his hand. "Hey, I'm sorry."

Tonya smiled. "I apologize, myself."

"Now that's what I'm talking about," Summer said. She was happy that the tension was gone, but she knew Tonya, and she could tell there was no chance that Ditty was going to get any pussy.

The waitress arrived with sweet teas for everybody. Tommy and Summer played under the table. Summer had his dick out in her hand, stroking it. Tommy couldn't believe that shit, but hey, they'd had sex in the men's restroom before. With Summer, anything could happen at anytime. It had been only two hours since they'd had phone sex. He couldn't believe she was still horny. He could feel himself getting aroused. He moved her hand and zipped his pants back up.

"Nigga, what you smiling for?" Ditty asked.

Tommy hesitated before speaking. "You know what? I think you and Tonya would make a great couple."

"Hell, yeah. I was just thinking the same thing."

Tonya turned to Ditty. She didn't say anything, but the look on her face said it all. It was like he stunk or something. He wasn't good enough for her.

Summer tried to pull Tommy's dick out again.

Tommy slapped her hands then announced, "I got to use the bathroom."

"Me too," Summer said.

"Yeah, ho. Go wash your damn hands." Tonya laughed.

When Summer and Tommy were gone, Ditty asked, "What's with the attitude?"

Tonya turned and faced him. "Nigga, I don't know you, so therefore I don't owe you no damn explanation."

"I mean, at least be nice."

"I'm being nice," she said, then folded her arms and turned away.

"Why did you come anyway, if you were going to be anti-social?"

Tonya sucked her teeth. "Just doing a friend a favor. That's all."

Ditty turned his head away, wondering why he came in the first place. It was always the fine ones that acted so stuck up. He looked at the next table. An old white couple was sharing a plate of french fries.

Tommy and Summer reappeared, smiling. Tonya made eye contact with Summer. "I'm ready to leave."

"What?" Tommy said angrily. "We haven't even begun to eat yet."

"I'm ready to go too, nigga." Ditty stood and Tonya scooted from the booth. Her perfume lingered and Ditty wondered why in the hell she had to be so damned difficult. Damn, he wanted to fuck her.

Tonya clutched her handbag tightly. "So" you going or what?"

"Yeah," Summer said, looking in Tommy's eyes. "I have to take her home."

Tommy dug into his pocket, pulled out a one-hundred dollar bill and offered it to Tonya. She didn't accept.

"What is this for?"

"Catch a cab home."

She flung her hair over her shoulders and stuck her chest out. She didn't say anything, but her expression said that catching a taxi was beneath her and that Ditty wasn't on her level.

Summer grabbed Tommy's hand and they made eye contact. "Tommy, I really have to take her home."

"What? Are you fuckin' this bitch? I want to see you, and just because she's acting like a Nazi""

Summer massaged Tommy's hand. "Come on, Tommy. Why would you say something like that?"

Tommy pulled his hand away. "I mean, you taking her side."

"Tommy I ain't taking nobody's side, but I have to take my girlfriend home."

"Call me later."

Summer leaned forward and kissed Tommy on his jaw.

J.C. was smiling when the younger teller flirted with him. He knew she didn't want him, but it was always good for his ego when he could catch the eye of a young woman""especially when the woman was so damned sexy. Jessica, the young Hispanic teller, had an ass that you could have a card tournament on. "Mr. Coleman, do you want large bills or small?"

J.C. smiled, revealing his newly capped teeth. He liked to show off his smile. One of the first things he did when he was awarded his money was to get his smile fixed. $18,000""sixteen caps and four veneers later he had a perfect smile.

Now J.C. walked out of the bank with an envelope containing $8,000. The bank had given him an equity credit line. His plans were to catch up on some of his bills with the money, and he would, but first he would have to call his supplier. He wanted to get high and he needed to get high fast. He opened the door of his Jeep Cherokee, pulled out his cell phone and dialed his supplier. Fifteen minutes later he arrived at his supplier's drug house. The man peeked through the curtains and minutes later he and J.C. were face to face. The supplier had a Crown Royal bag in his hand, which he opened. It contained small packages of coke.

J.C. pushed it away. "I want weight."

The man looked surprised. "What the hell are you talking about? You're a fuckin' crack head."

J.C. wanted to dispute it, but he couldn't. It was the truth. He hated words like crack head, junkie, and addict. He hated his addiction too, but he couldn't help it. He had to have a fix.

"So, what you gonna do, old man? Are you going to get some of this fire, or no?" The dealer dug into the bag and pulled out three baggies of coke. "This is the shit, man. I'm telling you, you better get it before I'm out."

JC looked the man in the eye. He couldn't tell if he was serious or not. He didn't know. He knew that dealers were like car salesmen. They bluffed a lot. He had plans to meet with a young escort tonight and party. "Hey. Couldn't you just sell me an ounce one time?"

"What's the point?"

"I can get more for my money."

"I will sell you four eight balls for $800."

J.C. walked back to his car. Then he turned back to the dealer and said, "I'll take it. And if you got any pills, I'll take a few of them, too."

The dealer smiled then disappeared into the house and came back out with the pills. The exchange was made.

10

Inside his hotel room at the Westin, J.C. waited on Shantelle, the $750 an hour escort. He dug into his pocket and pulled out three Cialis tablets. He wondered if he could get his dick up today. The last few times that he'd seen her, he hadn't been able to get it up without the help of Cialis. He quickly dismissed the thought of the Cialis, not because he didn't need it, but because he knew he'd be smoking crack later that night. He didn't know if his heart could take it at his age.

When Shantelle arrived, she was wearing a black, backless dress with 5-inch heels, making her already long legs appear longer. When she walked inside the room, she greeted J.C. with a hug. He grinned, thinking, this young bitch looks spectacular.

Shantelle walked past him. He examined her incredible body once again. Her waist was so damn tiny, and her ass just bubbled out like two cantaloupes. She was twenty-four and in incredible shape. She had been a track star, but lost her scholarship because her grades had dropped. She walked over to the bed, grabbed the remote and turned on the television. Crossing her legs, she revealed her muscular calves and beautiful toes. She asked, "So, do you want to handle our business first, Daddy?"

J.C. frowned. He knew she wanted to get paid first. Every time she'd come to see him she wanted her money up front. She'd seen him six times, and every time she wanted to get the payment out of the way. He pulled the bank envelope from his pocket, counted out seven $100 bills, two twenties, and a ten.

Shantelle was smiling and J.C. wondered what she was thinking. Did she think he was weak? Did she think he was an old fool? Or was she simply happy she would make $750 in one hour? There was a time when he wouldn't have given a dime to women, but then that was a time when he was working as a janitor. He desired pretty women, but he knew women were attracted to money, and at that time he simply didn't have it.

He handed her the money and she disappeared to the bathroom carrying her bag. When she reappeared, she was wearing a tiny silver G-string with a pair of clear, 5-inch heels. Her breasts sat upright and she was wearing a wig.

J.C. turned the TV off and eased over to the other side of the room. He sat in a chair next to the window and opened the curtain. He wanted to think someone could see them. This turned him on in a weird way.

When Shantelle walked, she swayed, sex appeal oozed as she looked at him seductively. She licked her full lips. J.C. unzipped his pants and pulled his dick out. She got on her knees and stroked it, but it still wouldn't rise.

J.C. felt embarrassed. He tried to concentrate to make it work, he looked at her brilliant ass again and her beautiful face, and remembered the last time they'd had sex. He had used Cialis and fucked her on the balcony, and she was screaming so hard he had to put a towel in her mouth. Even with his vivid imagination he couldn't make it rise.

"I'm sorry," he said.

She looked up at him as if she were glad, and he figured she probably was glad she didn't have to fuck an old man and happy she had made a quick $750. But he wouldn't let her off that easy. "Baby, I want to rub baby oil on that ass of yours. Maybe that will get it up."

She rose from the floor, kissed him on the jaw and winked. "Anything for you, Daddy."

Shantelle disappeared into the bathroom and reappeared wearing a yellow G-string that contrasted with her dark skin wonderfully. One thing was for damn sure; the young woman was sexy as hell, and this fact made J.C. even more frustrated. How could his dick not perform for her. He could feel himself rise, and when his dick was fully erect, she put the baby oil on the floor and got on her knees, again taking him in her mouth. She spat on his instrument and continued to suck until he wanted to stick it inside her. His condom was inside his wallet and he quickly dug, trying to come up with it before his erection went down. He had the purple Trojan packet in his hand and he ripped into it with his teeth, spit the condom packet out and slid the condom on. Meanwhile, Shantelle had peeled her underwear off. Her thong was now under the heel of her shoe. She turned her ass toward him. He looked at the tattoo of a rose at the small of her back. This young bitch is going to get it now, he told himself.

She smiled at him then licked her lips and opened her pussy.

When he pushed himself inside, she was wet. He sat back on the chair and she began to ride him, and he slapped that ass.

"Oh, Daddy."

"Damn, slow down," J.C. said.

"This dick is so good," she said.

Again J.C. looked at her tattoo and when he pulled her hair, he saw her facial expressions. Two minutes later he came and Shantelle didn't know. She kept throwing herself into him until his dick slipped out.

She turned and asked, "Was it good?"

Reluctantly, he shook his head. "Yeah. It was good," he said, but the fantasy was far better than the reality. This was always the case. In sex and in life. He knew this, but he was weak. He was a fiend for pussy, drugs, and a good time. He didn't want this lifestyle, but he had accepted that he'd been wired to like this. His father had died of alcoholism and chasing women and he figured if he didn't get a grip on himself, he probably would, too.

Shantelle was in the shower. He picked up his pants that were lying on the floor, and the bank envelope in his back pocket. He counted his money again. He'd spent $1,000 on the coke, the room was $140, and he'd given Shantelle $750. "Damn!" He cursed himself. He couldn't believe he'd become so weak.

Steam was coming from the bathroom. J.C. glanced at the door. He was now disgusted with Shantelle. Why in the hell couldn't she take a shower at home? She hummed some song by Usher. J.C. didn't know the name of the song, but he knew he'd heard it before.

"Daddy!" Shantelle yelled.

"Yeah. What do you want?" J.C. asked. He walked over to the table.

"Did you get something for me?"

He knew she was referring to the pills he'd bought for her. She loved pills and she loved him buying her pills. J.C. dug into his pocket, retrieved the pills and wondered why in the hell was he buying her pills when he had just given her $750.

Also in his pocket was his crack pipe, which was wrapped in aluminum foil. He pulled it out, broke off a piece of crack and put it on the end of the pipe. He flicked his lighter, trying desperately to light his pipe, but the lighter was dead. He had another in his jacket pocket. Inside the jacket pocket was a purple lighter. He flicked, and the flame was torch-like. The crack sizzled from the heat. J.C.'s heart rate increased. Damn. He felt good. He didn't have any worries. He liked feeling like this. The stench from the crack filled the room.

Shantelle yelled out, "Daddy, what you doing?"

J.C. didn't answer. The flame from the lighter burnt the tip of his finger and he let go of the button, paused for ten seconds, then lit the crack again.

Shantelle came out with a white hotel towel covering her body. J.C. didn't notice her. He just kept holding his torch as he sat in the chair.

Shantelle quickly closed the curtain. He was still flicking away. She dropped to her knees, pulled J.C.'s manhood from his boxer's and placed it in her mouth again. He glanced at her and wanted to tell her to stop but it was so pleasurable"¦ intense. He enjoyed the feeling though his heart pounded violently.

Country nudged Q when he saw the two women enter the margarita bar. "Hey, ain't that the bitch that was with your boy Tommy the other day in the park?"

Q lowered his Versace frames and peered over at the woman with the tight revealing dress. He strained his eyes to see what kind of panties she had on. In his mind he pictured her in black thongs. For a second he imagined him hitting her doggy style. "You know what? I don't know and I don't care. If she walks toward me, I'ma holla at her."

"Don't let her know that you know Tommy."

Q shrugged. "I don't give a fuck about him. All I know is my nigga is downtown because he was driving a car that nigga sold him."

Country nodded his head in agreement then drank his water. He really didn't care for margaritas. He always figured they were for girls.

Seconds later, a thin waitress appeared at the table. Her name tag read Meagan. She smiled a bright smile and asked, "Are you guys okay? Do you need anything else to drink?"

Q pulled out a wad of money then pointed to the two black women on the other side of the room. "Here is a hundred for you"¦" He lowered his glasses and beamed in on her name tag ""¦Meagan, and I want you to take this other hundred to the women across the room. Tell them that I'm covering their drinks for the rest of the evening."

Meagan put the money in her apron. "Thanks a lot." She disappeared to the other side of the room. She told the women what Q said. Both women waved and smiled.

Q held his cool and winked.

The two women walked over to the table and introduced themselves. The lighter skinned woman offered her hand. "Hi. My name is Summer and this is my friend Tonya."

Q held her hand for a long time. He looked at her face

and realized Country was right. This was Tommy's girlfriend. Damn. This bitch is bad, he thought.

"I'm Quentin, and this is my boy, Country."

Country smiled at Tonya but she turned her head.

"Have a seat," Q offered.

When Summer sat down, she crossed her legs, and Q couldn't help but stare. He wondered how in the hell did a fat ass like Tommy have a woman like this. Then he realized it had to be the money. His mission was to show them that Q had money too. He held his platinum Rolex watch up for a long time, wanting everybody to look at it, before finally saying, "I didn't realize it was so late."

"It's only six," Tonya said.

"It's late for me because I've been working all morning."

Summer smiled then asked. "What is that you do?"

"Music business."

"Rapper?"

"No, executive. I have two artists and I just inked a multi-million dollar distribution deal."

"With who?" Tonya asked.

Q looked at her with suspicion. He didn't want to say the wrong thing. He knew a lot of those groupie gold-digging chicks knew about music and record companies. "I don't understand your question." Q stalled for time.

"Who is your distribution deal with?"

"Hood America Records""a subsidiary of Virgin."

Tonya shook her head. Her face said she didn't believe him but she simply said, "Impressive."

"Thank you."

"So can we be in a video?" Summer asked.

Q's mind went straight to the gutter. Oh yeah you definitely can be in my video, he thought, as he pictured himself sexing her from behind with his video camera going.

"So, do you have a boyfriend?" Q asked Summer.

Summer shrugged her shoulders. "Kind of."

"How can you kind of have a boyfriend?"

Summer put her hands over his lips. "Shhh. Let's not talk about him."

"Fine with me."

Country turned to Tonya who was looking like she was bored.

"So what ya'll got planned for the evening?"

Summer toyed with her hair then wrapped her full lips around the straw in the margarita glass. Q's dick stiffened as he thought of her giving him head.

"Nothing; we're just chillin'" having a few drinks."

"Where are you from?" Q asked.

She smiled. "Texas" but I have been here for about four years."

"I can tell you weren't from here."

She frowned. "What you trying to say? I'm country? This ain't hardly the city."

"No I ain't trying to say you country. Calm you nerves. I'm just saying you sound different." Q massaged her hands and looked into her eyes. "I like it actually."

Tonya turned and laughed. "She don't like nobody calling Texas the country."

Q strategically placed his hands on the table so the women could look at his canary yellow diamond ring, then he faced Tonya, who was looking down at the table. "So, you feeling my man Country? Because he was the one that spotted ya'll" particularly you."

"Why can't he talk for himself?" Tonya asked.

Country had always been kind of clumsy around women. Q was the ladies' man. He had the talk and the game. He had always been responsible for Country's girlfriends. Country wasn't an ugly guy, but he had no talk" no game, and women didn't like the fact that his conversation was whack.

Q smiled and then pulled his Versace sunglasses from his pocket and placed them over his eyes. Again, this was done purposely. He knew they wanted getting-money type niggas. "My boy has his mind on his paper, that's all."

"Ain't nothing wrong with that," Summer said.

"I can talk for myself," Country finally said.

"Do you like what you see?" Tonya asked.

"Hell yeah."

"Let's go back to my penthouse," Q said.

"We don't know ya'll like that," Summer said.

"Listen, baby, I ain't no serial killer. You are safe with Q."

"Is that what they call you?"

Damn. Q didn't mean to let his nickname slip out. He knew she was Tommy's bitch and if ever Tommy discussed him, it would be easy to realize who he was.

"Yeah some people call me Q, but I prefer the ladies to call me Quentin because that's what my mama calls me."

"You a mama's boy, huh?"

"Something like that."

"Yeah, that nigga's a mama's boy. His mama still cooks for him. She prepares his food for the week," Country said.

"Ah, how sweet," Tonya said.

"That's a good thing. It means you respect women," Summer said.

I wouldn't say all that, Q thought. He glanced at Summer's toned calves. He pictured himself fucking her on his balcony, pulling her hair and smacking her ass.

"So, can I call you?" Q asked her.

She blushed and then said, "I don't know. It depends."

"Depends on what?" Q asked. He knew he had more money than Tommy, and he knew he was more charming and good looking. What the hell could it depend on? he thought.

"If you're a player."

"You have a boyfriend, ma. What you talking about?"

"I don't exactly have a boyfriend."

"First of all, that player shit ain't me."

"Yeah, right," she said, smiling.

"Seriously. That's old and I'm about to be thirty next year."

Summer pulled out her cell phone, smiled politely and asked, "Quentin, let me have your number. I think it will be better that way."

"I understand," Q said, then he spit out his digits.

11

Squirt was in his cell reading his Bible. He had sworn to God that if he got out of this one, he would get a job and spend more time with his son and his baby's mother. He thought about all those nights when he ran the street and never spent time with Sheniqua, or his little boy. He looked up at the aluminum bed and read the words etched in the bed""This is Hell. He had to agree with whoever authored the phrase. This was hell, and he didn't want to be here. He remembered the white arresting officer saying, if ever he wanted to help himself, give him a call. He knew the man meant snitching. He couldn't do that, nor would he ever do it. It went against his morals, unless somebody was a child molester or cold-blooded killer, but even then his life or his kid's safety would have to be in direct danger. He hated being in jail and it seemed as if ever since he was 16 years old he'd gone to jail at least once a year for one thing or another. But now he was twenty-three, and he had gotten caught with nine ounces of crack cocaine. With his record, this could give him ten years. If the feds picked up the case, he could get life. God, please don't let the feds pick up my case. If the feds got the case, he knew he was bound to be gone until his two-year-old son was about to finish high school, and he didn't want that. He pulled out the pink paperwork with his charges on it. When he did, Jessie, an old con, walked into the cell. Jessie was 46-years-old with graying braids in his hair.

The two men made eye contact before Jessie said, "Put that paperwork up, young buck."

"Why?"

"Nigga, there're a lot of snitches dying to look at your paperwork to get out of jail." Jessie's face hardened. "Remember that."

Squirt knew Jessie was telling the truth, because he'd been to jail before. He folded his paperwork. "There's nobody in here but us."

"I don't wanna see nobody's paperwork, because I don't want to even see mine." Jessie sat on the edge of the desk. Then he pulled out a carton of lemonade that was left from lunch. He opened it and took a sip. "This shit is the pits. Ain't it, man?"

Squirt sat up on the edge of his bed. "I was just thinking, man, if I ever get out of this one, I'm finished with this shit."

"Yeah, I know what ya mean. I've often promised God over the years, too."

"Jessie, I know you don't want to hear about my case, but I have to get somebody's opinion."

Jessie sat the carton down and took a deep breath. "Listen, man, I really don't need this shit. I got my own shit to worry about, and believe me, my shit is far worse than a petty-ass drug case."

Squirt looked surprised. "How do you know I have a drug case? I haven't told anybody."

"Doesn't take a rocket scientist to know that you're in here for a dope case. Most of these young boys in here are, and you ain't no different."

"What is that supposed to mean?"

Jessie stood, took off his orange jumpsuit, got his deodorant and toothpaste and soap. "Man, I have to get in the shower before they lock down."

"We got an hour."

"Yeah but everybody is going to want to take a shower at the same time."

"Jessie, I do have a dope case and I think somebody set me up."

Jessie looked Squirt square in the face. "You set yourself up, young buck."

"What is that supposed to mean?"

"It mean you thought you could make a living off that shit and it only takes one time for the cops to get you and it's over. Did you really think about the risk?"

Squirt thought hard. He hadn't ever thought about the risk. He didn't care about the risk. He thought about the money he needed, his son needed, his baby's mother needed, but he knew what they needed most was him. "You right, Jessie."

Jessie walked toward the door. Before he could open it, Squirt asked, "How many people in here are for drugs?"

"I would say, out of the 54 people in here, 45 are in here for drugs. There's a couple of child molesters in here, too."

Squirt put his hand behind his head as he lay back on the bed. "Jessie, what you in here for?"

Jessie stepped back inside the cell, closed the door tightly and looked Squirt directly in his eyes. "I'm in here for murder."

Squirt's eyes grew, but he didn't say anything.

"Yeah. A motherfucker raped my 14-year-old daughter and I took him out."

"Oh yeah?"

"I admitted to it. I mean, my lawyer and the DA understands it. I am trying to plead temporary insanity."

"How much time does it carry?"

"I can probably get fourteen because my record is fucked up."

Squirt took a deep breath. "I know what you mean," Squirt said, thinking of the two prior drug convictions he had on his record. Though he had never been to prison, he had been sent to boot camp, once, for ninety days.

"I have to get in the shower," Jessie said.

"Please listen to my story."

Jessie looked at Squirt again. His facial expression said he really didn't want to hear what Squirt had to say, but he sat on

"I'm telling you, man, I ain't have nothing to do with your man going to jail," Tommy said. He and Q were at a booth in the back of the Waffle House. It was 3:00 am and the restaurant was full of patrons from the strip clubs and other night spots.

Q stared at Tommy straight in his face. He was trying to see if Tommy was afraid, but Tommy didn't bat an eye. He wanted to believe Tommy, but all he knew was his man had gone to jail because of the car.

"Q, I don't have a case. What do I need to set your boy up for? And furthermore, that ain't my style."

"Do you know this is his third offense, Tommy?"

"Why the fuck do I need to know that? I mean, that's the risk when you deal, nigga. I mean, that's your boy. You better be worried; not me."

"It's your car, nigga."

"No, it's Squirt's car," Tommy said with a serious face.

Two strippers walked by wearing tight fitting jeans and heels. Q grabbed the shorter of the two's ass and the woman turned around and said, "Motherfucker!" She stopped in mid-sentence and smiled. "Oh. Hey, Q."

"What's up Diamond?"

"Not much. Will you pay for me and Passion's food?"

Q tossed her a hundred. "Wait for me in the parking lot. I want to hang out with you tonight."

She smiled. "Okay."

Q slapped Passion on the ass too. "I want you to hang out with us."

Passion didn't respond. She just followed Diamond.

Q leaned across the table. "Tommy, how did you come home so fast from the feds?"

"I did my time."

"Nigga, you were a kingpin."

"Yeah, and what is that supposed to mean?"

"You should have got thirty."

Tommy's face became hard. "Q, what the fuck are you trying to say?"

Q looked away. The waitress dropped two plates of walnut waffles on the table.

"Q, what the fuck are you trying to say?"

"I'm just asking, Tommy. No need to get uptight."

Tommy poured some syrup on his waffles. He knew that there were some people on the streets that thought he was an informant because he'd had so much money and he had gotten out of prison early. He really didn't care what they thought, as long as he knew he had done the right thing, and the right thing to him was sticking to his morals and never snitching on his boys. Now that he was out of prison he didn't know if he could go back on a drug case. That's why he chose to stay away from drugs.

"Listen, Tommy, man, I'm sorry. I shouldn't have said that."

"Q, I'm really offended man. I mean, my case was publicized. Yeah, I testified on a DEA officer""the bitch that sat me up. That's how I got out of jail. Never did I tell on anybody that did anything with me."

Q drank his orange juice slowly. "I know. I remember hearing about the case."

"Well, why in the fuck did you ask me did I have your boy fucked up, Q?"

"All I know is my man is in jail and he said it was because of your car."

"He said my car caused him to go to jail?"

"Yeah. Said the paperwork wasn't right."

"I have nothing to do with the paperwork."

"You sold us the car. Right?"

Tommy put his hand over his mouth. "Shh. Quiet."

"You sold us the car."

"Listen, nigga, I don't even know your boy's name, so how in the fuck am I gonna set him up?"

Q was quiet. Tommy had brought up a good point. Diamond tapped on the window. When Q looked up, Diamond licked her lips. He held up his hand indicating he wanted her to hold on for five minutes.

"Q, man, you gotta believe me. I didn't have nothing to do with this."

"I hope not, Tommy. I like you. I like you a lot, but if I find out that you did, I'ma have to put in work."

"What the fuck is that supposed to mean?"

Q stood, tossed $100 on the table and said, "Tommy, I hope this shit is not what I think."

Tommy stood. He'd made up his mind he had to be ready for war, because nobody was going to threaten him; nobody was going to make him out to be a snitch. He wasn't scared of Q, or anybody else for that matter.

12

DEA agent Mark Pratt walked into the interrogation room. He waited ten minutes in the cold room, with only his legal pad in his hand. He looked at the suspect's jacket. Jerome Miller was a 22-year-old black man. He'd had two prior drug cases""nothing substantial. Pratt figured he was a petty criminal and he knew that Miller might want to save his own ass once he knew the case was going federal. Cooperating with the feds in this case might save the young man seven years. Miller walked in a tad shorter than the 5'6" height indicated on his arrest record. The Mecklenburg County jumpsuit swallowed his thin frame. Pratt offered his hand.

Miller didn't shake it. He sat down across from Pratt. "Yeah, who are you?"

Pratt pulled out his DEA badge. "I'm with the DEA."

"Okay. What do you want with me?"

"Your case is going federal."

Squirt looked surprised. "Nine ounces is going federal? What, are you crazy?"

"You had a gun and the ATF will be seeking an indictment."

"Come on, man. Are you serious?"

Squirt cracked his knuckles. He was nervous, but he tried his best to remain calm.

"So, what you want from me?"

"Just wanting to know if you wanted to help yourself."

"You want me to tell?"

Pratt shrugged his shoulders and said, "That's totally up to you. You're facing thirty with the gun and the dope, so if you want to get out before you rot in prison"|'"

"I ain't got nothing to say."

Pratt dropped his pen on his pad. There was a long silence in the cold room. He stared at the young man across from him. His eyes were sincere; he would never tell. He was the kind that made Pratt's job harder. He had seen many kinds of criminals over the years and he had become pretty good at sizing them up. He knew there was no use in pressing the issue.

Jerome cracked his knuckles again and then looked away from Pratt and stared at the bright yellow wall as if he were contemplating. Pratt figured the walls were closing in on him.

"What ya thinking about?"

Jerome turned and faced Pratt. He started to speak but hesitated. Finally he said, "My little boy."

Pratt picked up his pen and scribbled a squiggly line to see if the pen wrote. It did. Maybe he'd been wrong about Jerome. Maybe he would cooperate after all. "You have a family, huh?"

Jerome looked irritated. "Of course I have a family."

"They deserve you to be there for them."

"I know."

"How old is your son?"

"He's two."

"I have a newborn." Pratt smiled proudly.

"Congrats."

"Thank you." It was an odd moment; two men talking about their kids. At that moment, both men were proud parents'"'not cop and bad guy.

"You love your son a lot. Don't you?"

Jerome hesitated before answering. Again he stared at the

walls. The room seemed colder and the chill bumps gathered on his arms. This was the kind of room that could break a man down. "What kind of question is that?"

"Just asking."

"Of course I love my son."

"Well do it for him."

"I want my son to be proud."

Pratt smiled then pulled out a picture of his son. A little boy in a sailor suit with blue blocks that spelled baby. He handed Jerome the picture.

Jerome smiled. "What's his name?"

"Charles."

"Charles? That name is for an older person."

"I know. My wife's father's name was Charles, so we went with it."

Jerome passed the picture back to Pratt.

Pratt dropped the pen on the pad again. "Are you going to help yourself?"

"No."

"What about your son?"

"I want him to be proud."

"I don't understand."

"I want him to know that his pops stood for something."

"You're a dope dealer."

"I made a mistake"¦okay?"

Pratt stood up, grabbed the pen, put the top back on it then placed it behind his ear. He picked up the pad. "You have a good day, Jerome." He turned to walk out of the room.

"Agent Pratt"¦" Jerome called out.

Mark turned and faced Jerome. They stared at each other for a while until Jerome broke the silence. "Did Tommy Dupree tell on me?"

Mark squinted his eyes. He'd heard the name before but he couldn't remember where he knew the name from.

Mark shrugged his shoulders. "I don't know who the informant on this case was, and if I did, I couldn't tell you."

Jerome stood. Then a black female correctional officer walked in to escort Jerome back to his cell. "Pratt, you know

I'ma find out who did this to me."

Mark didn't say anything. He just looked and wondered why the name Tommy Dupree seemed familiar to him. And when Jerome was gone, he remembered. Tommy Dupree was an ecstasy dealer whom he'd investigated six years ago; he was sentenced to prison. Was he out? Mark wondered. The yellow walls closed in on him.

Tommy's eyes rolled into the back of his head. He continued to stroke, trying not to break the bed. He held the bed rail. Angie looked up at him with anticipation. She moved her body with Tommy's. It had become hard because Tommy had no rhythm. She kissed his neck. "Baby, right there"¦that's my spot!" she screamed.

"Damn, your pussy is so wet."

"You like this?" Angie asked with her fingernails on his back. She clawed his back. It was very painful for Tommy, but at the same time he liked it.

"I love this shit," Tommy said. He was trying to keep up the pace but he was out of shape and it was starting to show.

"Keep hitting this pussy."

Tommy let go of the bed rail and wiped his face. The sweat was streaming down his face into his eyes and lips. It was salty and his eyes burned.

She bit on his neck and played with his nipples. He liked when she did this.

"Baby, I want to cum inside this pussy."

"Don't cum inside me."

Tommy started to breathe heavy and she tried to push him off her but he was too heavy.

"Tommy please don't cum inside me. I don't want to get pregnant."

His whole body jerked. He came inside her. He was out of breath. She managed to push him off her. "Damn it, Tommy"¦ why the fuck did you do that?" Angie ran to the shower. She would shower fast. Her mother had told her that if she showered soon after sex it would cut down on the chance of a pregnancy.

She didn't know if she believed that or not but she knew it was worth a try.

Tommy stood, walked into the steaming bathroom to grab a towel from the closet then wiped himself off. "Baby, I'm sorry."

She pulled the shower curtain back. "Fuck you, Tommy. You trying to get me pregnant?"

"What's wrong with that?"

"What's wrong with it, nigga? What's right with it?"

Tommy wiped himself off. "I'm offended. You act like the worst thing in the world is to be pregnant by me."

"Tommy, you're still out there hustling."

"I'm not selling dope."

She pulled the curtains back again. "What is that supposed to mean?"

"It means that I'm not going back to jail."

"You don't know that."

The thought of going back to jail made him say a prayer.

Tommy sat on the toilet seat and held his face in his hands. He knew she didn't want his child and this made him sad.

"Tommy!" she called out.

He didn't respond. He just sat there wondering would he ever give his father a grandson. Would he ever have a child of his own?

"Tommy."

He finally looked toward the shower curtain. She rinsed herself off and hopped out of the shower, walking right by him. He didn't make eye contact with her. She got a large pink towel and began to dry off.

"So why don't you just admit it, Angie?"

"Admit what, Tommy?"

"Admit you don't want kids with me."

"Not right now, Tommy."

"So, what's the point of this relationship?"

She held up her hand. "Tommy I don't see a ring on my finger. You haven't asked me to marry you."

Tommy stood up from the toilet, stepped back into the bedroom and put his shorts on.

"Tommy, why the hell are you avoiding that question?"

"Marriage has nothing to do with babies."

"Tommy, I don't want to be no damn baby's mama."

"Is that what this is all about? Marriage?"

She walked out of the bathroom, still butt naked; body glistening from baby oil. Tommy looked at her ass but then turned away. He was mad and he had to remember that. She opened a drawer and got out a white G-string. From the top of the closet she got some sweatpants then sat on the edge of the bed. "Tommy, I want to get married one day. What girl doesn't?"

"I wanna get married, too."

"Why haven't you asked me?"

"I'ma ask you when I want to ask you," he said, looking away.

"Well, just like your pops keep asking you when you going to have some kids, my mama keeps asking me when we are going to get married. She says I'm twenty-eight, like I'm a old-ass maid."

"I'm not ready to get married yet."

"And I ain't ready to be nobody's baby's mama, either."

Tommy reached for his pants on the floor. Angie grabbed his hand, trying to keep him from putting on his pants, but she couldn't. He removed her hand from his wrist then put his clothes on and left.

13

Q gave little Eddie sixteen packets. "Here. Go stash this." Eddie looked at Q like he didn't want to do it.

"What the fuck is wrong with you, nigga? I said go stash this."

Eddie put the packs in his pockets and walked away slowly before Q called out, "Eddie, what's wrong with you?"

Eddie turned and faced Q. He was nervous, as most were nervous when Q spoke. Everybody knew he was a loose cannon and would snap at anytime. Eddie hesitated before speaking. "Q, it's just that we are moving so much product that it makes no sense for me to go stash this. I mean, you'll probably be sending me for this shit in a few minutes."

"What the fuck is your point, nigga?" Q walked toward him. "Motherfucker, I'm the boss. Have you forgotten who pays you?"

"No, Q."

Q looked Eddie in his eyes. He could tell he was afraid, and he knew Eddie was no match for him. Though Eddie was taller than Q, he was lanky, very young, and inexperienced. Because he was younger, they called him little; not because of his size. Q thought of Eddie as a good soldier that always did what he was told. He really didn't want to hurt him, but he had to let him know that nobody should question his authority. Country and Stickman, another member of the crew, looked on. Q didn't want nobody to think he was soft. It would send the wrong message. "Eddie, go stash the motherfuckin' dope before I backhand your ass."

"Don't talk to me like that, Q," Eddie said trembling, with sweat coming down his forehead.

Q lifted up his shirt revealing his gun. "What, motherfucker? You want to try me?"

"No, Q I was just saying don't talk to me disrespectful."

Q took a step toward Eddie. Country and Stickman grabbed Q. "Take it easy."

"Get the fuck off me." Q broke free from the two men and walked toward Eddie.

"I don't want no problems, man." Eddie licked his chapped lips and swallowed hard.

"Go stash the motherfuckin' dope then, nigga."

Eddie ran away through the path, fast. He put the dope in a tunnel across from a ditch.

Danny, the white boy, came up carrying two laptop computers""one Dell and one Apple. "Q, can I talk to you?"

"Danny, I don't want no damn computers."

"They are new; fresh out the box."

Q's face hardened. "What the fuck am I going to do? Go on Myspace or some shit?"

Danny laughed at Q's lighthearted humor. "Hey, Q, all I want is five rocks, man."

Stickman walked up to Q. "Hey, my sister needs a laptop. She's away at school."

Q turned to Country. "How much money we done made out here today?"

"I would say around twelve G's."

"Gimme the computers."

Danny passed the computers to Q, who turned to Stickman.

"You know this shit coming out of your pay. Right, nigga?"

"It's fine."

"Write that shit down, Country," Q ordered like a true businessman. He kept track of everything and he never took shorts.

Lil' Eddie showed up seconds later and Q said, "Go back. Get the stash."

Eddie shook his head and disappeared back into the path.

14

Mark Pratt ran Tommy Dupree's name. According to records, he had been released from BOP almost eighteen months ago. Mark stared at the picture and remembered how Tommy had gotten off easy. He wondered if Tommy was up to his old tricks. Of course he was up to his old tricks. Jerome had been caught with nine ounces of coke, and he believed that Tommy had ratted him out. One thing Mark knew about Tommy is that he was not the informant type. But he couldn't tell Jerome this. He would find Tommy and observe him a bit. Though he wasn't on the radar, Mark still wanted to know what he was up to.

According to county records, Tommy lived at 3830 Windsor Place, a very affluent neighborhood in the southeastern part of town. Mark rode down the long winding street until he finally saw 3830""a huge single-level home with a garage"|nothing out of the ordinary. He drove down to the end of the cul-de-sac then turned around. When he was coming back past the house he noticed a black Range Rover pulling out of the driveway.

He recognized the man immediately. It was Tommy Dupree. He looked the same. Tommy backed out of the driveway and whisked away. Mark trailed him and wondered what Tommy was up to. Was he wrong for suspecting that he was involved in illegal activity? Was he wrong for targeting him? Was he just curious? His mind told him that it was a vendetta that he'd had against Tommy because Tommy had gotten away. He continued to trail him by about two car lengths until Tommy turned into Ballantyne Commons Parkway. The Range Rover disappeared into some town homes. Mark drove in among the town homes. He didn't see Tommy right away. He spotted him after noticing a black 745 BMW with 24-inch chrome wheels parked on the side of the street. Tommy was parked behind the car talking to a black man with braids and a whole lot of tacky gold jewelry. The men talked for a few moments then the other man got into the car with Tommy and drove across the street to McAllister's deli. They went inside the restaurant.

Inside the restaurant, Ditty and Tommy waited in a corner on Jay and Matt. Neither man had anything to eat. Tommy said, "I swear to you, I was being followed."

"Followed? By who?" Ditty asked.

"I don't know. I saw this silver Dodge Magnum in my neighborhood trailing me. Whoever it was followed me until I turned into your neighborhood."

"You think it was one of Q's boys?"

"Them niggas don't know where I live."

"We need to handle that shit, man. We can't let them niggas think that we're pussies."

"They ain't gonna do shit."

"Tommy, they think you set Squirt up."

Just the thought of having another black man locked up made Tommy mad.

"I know you didn't do it, and I know them niggas know you didn't have him set up."

"How did he get locked up?"

"I don't know. Maybe the nigga did something stupid;

maybe an improper lane change and they smelled marijuana on him."

"We have to find out his last name."

"How?"

"We have to go to his hood and ask around," Tommy said.

"Where does he live?"

"I don't know, but I know where Q is from."

"He's probably from Q's hood."

"That would be my guess too."

Tommy swallowed hard but didn't say anything. He thought about going to Q's hood. He thought about how loyal Q's people were. If he were spotted, there could be problems.

"What's wrong, Tommy?"

"I don't want problems, man. I know if one of those niggas threaten me it's gonna be problems."

"I don't give a fuck about Q. I don't like his punk ass anyway."

Jay and Matt walked up to the table. They sat across from Tommy and Ditty. "I got a new Escalade. It's white." Matt said.

Tommy was thinking somebody had said they wanted an Escalade but he couldn't remember. He wanted to buy the car because he knew that he could easily sell it, but he had to wonder if the feds were on to the cars. How did Squirt get caught? Something wasn't right. He reached over the table and frisked Matt.

"What the hell are you doing?" Matt asked.

"Checking for wires."

Matt laughed then lifted his shirt, and so did Jay. "Tommy, you're fuckin' crazy, man. What the hell have you been smoking?"

Tommy's face was stern. A few seconds later he laughed. "Hey, man, I'm sorry. I just have to be careful. I don't want to go to jail."

"Hell, me either," Matt said.

"Something ain't right," Tommy said.

"What are you talking about?"

"I'm talking about the guy I sold the car to going to jail."

"It has nothing to do with us, man. I've sold twenty cars

since we last talked," Matt said.

Ditty said, "We're just being careful, that's all."

"So when can I get the Escalade?" Tommy asked. He needed to make some money. He hadn't sold any cars since Squirt had been busted. But who would he sell to? Q and his crew thought he was the police. He would get the vehicle and worry about details later.

"I can get it to you in an hour," Matt said confidently.

"Is it new?"

"Twenty-six thousand miles on it," Matt said.

"What do you want for it?" Tommy asked.

"Thirty thousand."

"Twenty-five, you got yourself a deal."

15

Tommy called his pop's name out when he entered the house, but he didn't get a response. He went to the kitchen, but his dad wasn't there. He opened the bedroom door. He saw his father passed out lying across the bed with his boots still on. Tommy pulled his pop's boots off just like he did when he was a kid. He put him in the bed then covered him up. As he was about to walk out of the room he noticed a glass tube on the dresser. When he picked it up he immediately knew what it was" a crack pipe. What the hell was a crack pipe doing in his pop's house? Was his pops smoking? Then he thought hard. Maybe that's how he blew the money? He became angry. He grabbed J.C.'s shoulder and shook him. J.C. just grunted and turned over on his side but he would not wake. Tommy stared at his father for a long time. Could it be his hero was smoking crack? The man that showed him how to play baseball, taught him to fish"

Though J.C. wasn't Tommy's biological father, he was still the only father he knew. Tommy's cell phone rang. The caller ID read Matt. Tommy answered.

"Tommy, are you ready?"

"Just give me a few minutes."

"Okay, but I'm kind of pressed for time."

"I told you I was going to need two hours."

"Yeah I know. Where can we meet?"

"Carolina Place Mall."

"Okay. I will be there in forty-five minutes."

"Okay," Tommy said, terminating the call. He sat on the edge of the bed and held the crack pipe in his hand. He couldn't believe this was happening to him. His father was all he had. His mother had died years ago. Now his hero had let him down. The man who told him, "Don't ever do drugs," was doing drugs. Tommy wondered if this was a punishment from God for dealing all the years he'd dealt drugs. He'd sold drugs to mamas, daughters, fathers, and sons and maybe this was his payback. God, he hoped this was only a bad dream. Minutes had passed while he thought. The phone rang again. It was Matt.

"Yeah."

"What side of the mall do you want to meet me on?"

"The side where the Sears entrance is."

"Okay."

"I will probably beat you there. I'm about five minutes away."

"Okay. Just wait on me."

"I'll probably just step inside and get something to eat""probably at Sabarro's."

"Okay," Tommy said, then ended the call. He picked the crack pipe up again then dropped it on the carpet. With his shoe, he smashed it. He looked over at his dad, who was snoring now. He stood over him, kissed him, and left.

Tommy picked Ditty up in front of his house. Ditty made small talk, but Tommy's mind was still on his father and the crack pipe he'd found. This had to be one of the worst moments of his life. They stopped at a red light about a mile away from the mall. Tommy was in the center lane when the light turned green in the turning lane. He pulled out into the middle of traffic. A

Toyota Avalanche came to a screeching halt and a burly white man with a beard rolled down his window and yelled, "Watch what the fuck you're doing!"

Ditty had placed his hands on the dashboard to brace himself when Tommy stopped since Ditty was not wearing his seatbelt.

"What the hell are you doing, man?" Ditty said nervously.

Tommy weaved between a blue Dodge Intrepid and a white Honda Accord, barely missing the Accord. He then pulled to the side of the road and put the car in park. His heart beat fast. He looked at Ditty and said, "I'm sorry, man."

"What's wrong?"

"Nothing."

Ditty looked at Tommy who was avoiding his eyes. "Something is wrong. Your mind has been somewhere else since you picked me up."

"Nothing's wrong."

"Come on, man. You know I know you."

Tommy shifted into drive and pulled off. He didn't say another word on the way to the mall.

Tommy and Ditty found Matt and Jay in the food court, not in front of the Sabarro's like Matt had said, but in front of Chick-fil-A drinking lemonade and eating chicken sandwiches. Jay offered Tommy some fries as he walked up.

"No. I'm watching my figure," Tommy teased.

Matt and Jay stood while they continued to eat their food.

"Where did you park?"

"I came in through Sears like we'd talked about."

"Got the money?"

Tommy looked at him oddly. "Come on, man. We've been doing this shit for almost a year. You know I got the money."

Matt and Jay left the unfinished food on the table and they all walked through the food court to exit the mall. Matt handed Ditty the keys. Tommy got the Macy's shopping bag that contained the money out of the car and gave it to Jay.

"I'll count it and give you a call," Jay said.

"You know the money's right."

Jay smiled. "Lighten up, Tommy."

"I'm light enough"¦about twenty-five grand lighter."

The white boys pulled away in the Dodge Ram. Ditty had pulled away but had only driven a few feet in the new Escalade when Tommy called him on his cell phone. Ditty answered on the second ring. "Yeah."

"Stop."

"Stop? What do you mean, stop? We need to get the hell away from here."

"I want to get in the car with you."

Ditty stopped and Tommy locked his vehicle and walked toward the Escalade that was now in reverse. When Tommy got into the car, he looked serious and his eyes were now red. Ditty asked, "What's wrong?"

Tommy took a deep breath and looked toward the window; a few seconds of silence fell upon them. Finally, Tommy said, "I think my pops is smoking crack."

16

Q's caller ID read Squirt's baby mama. He answered it on the second ring.

"What up, nigga?" Squirt said.

Q was surprised when he heard his voice.

"When did you get out?"

"I'm not out. I'm still inside."

"You good? You need anything?"

"Just help my lady out every now and then with my son, and I will be okay."

"Cool. I got you. Don't even worry about it."

"Q, the feds came to see me."

"What? They came to see you for nine ounces? That ain't shit."

"I mean, I don't think they're going to take the case, but they wanted to know what I know. You know, the same ol' shit."

"Tryin' to get you to rat, huh?"

"Yeah, but you know that ain't me."

"Don't worry. I got you, dawg."

"Q, one other thing"¦that nigga Tommy ain't shit."

"What you mean?"

"He did this to me Q."

"Did they"¦the feds say it?"

"You know they ain't gone tell you that shit, but I asked."

"You have proof that he did this to you?"

"No, but I know he did. I just got a gut feeling he did it, Q."

"Don't worry. I will take care of that situation for you."

There was a long silence then an operator announced that there was one minute remaining in the phone conversation. Q asked, "Do you need anything else?"

"That's okay, Q. I'm good."

"Yo, just let me know nigga. I'm here for you. I'ma take your girl some paper over there."

"Appreciate it, man. She needs help with the phone bill."

"I gotcha, nigga."

The phone disconnected.

Mark Pratt trailed Tommy to a car wash on the west side of town. There Tommy and Ditty, who had also followed Tommy, met two men; both black. One was tall and skinny; the other one had a more solid build and was wearing a wife beater with tattoos covering his body. Mark sat across the street and watched. He wanted to know what was going on. Who were those men and what were they talking about? Questions needed to be answered. Tommy handed the tall skinny man the keys who then gave them to the man with the tattoos who then hopped into the Escalade. Why was this truck changing hands so much? The skinny guy gave Tommy a Nike shoe box. Tommy jumped into Ditty's car, and they pulled off.

Mark Pratt followed the men to the Bahaman apartment complex in the ghetto on the west side of Charlotte. He drove into the parking lot then quickly exited. There were no leads; only confusion. Who the hell were these men? Were they drug dealers? How would he find out? He would have to come back with help. He knew he was on to something. But what? he wondered. He turned his air conditioning unit up and drove away.

At his father's house, Tommy counted the money he'd received from Scooter. He sold the Escalade for thirty-five grand, profiting $10,000. After he counted the money, he climbed up into the attic. When he was coming down from the attic, he met J.C., who was smiling. "Hey, I didn't know you were here."

Tommy stepped down then pushed the ladder back up into the attic. He walked past J.C.

"What's wrong, son?"

Tommy ignored his father and headed for the door.

"Tommy, you don't see me?"

Tommy turned and faced him. They stared at each other for a while. Then Tommy walked past J.C. into the living room. He sat down on the sofa nearest the TV and crossed his legs. J.C. came in behind him. "Son, what is bothering you?"

Tommy looked. His father seemed thin, but maybe he'd always been that size. Maybe it was the fact that he'd seen the crack pipe that made him appear thinner. "Pops, earlier, when you were asleep"|" Tommy stopped.

"Son, what is it?"

"Pops, are you smoking that shit?"

J.C. lowered his gaze. He didn't answer. He walked over and sat on the sofa next to Tommy. "Hell, no. Are you crazy?"

"Well, what the hell happened to your money?"

"Bad investments, Tommy."

"Bullshit. You smoking and you know it."

"Watch how you talk to me, son. I'm still your daddy."

Tommy stood. He turned his back then said, "I'm outta here."

"Son, don't go."

Tommy turned and faced J.C. He noticed that his T-shirt was too big for his pop's frame. Now that he could see him, he realized he'd definitely lost weight.

"Pops, how could you do it?"

"Son, I wasn't"|"

"I saw the crack pipe."

"It wasn't mine," J.C. said as he turned from Tommy's gaze and started to walk away.

Tommy grabbed his pop's bony shoulders. "Oh, my God. Look how skinny you are."

J.C. turned and faced his son. His eyes were now red. "Son, I ain't gonna bullshit you."

"I'm listening."

"I have a problem"¦I mean, I tried"¦I mean, shit's been hard."

Tommy threw his arms up in disgust. "Shit hasn't been that fuckin' hard. How in the hell could you do this?"

"Son, the money brought the problems and the problems brought the stress."

"But YOU bought the fuckin' crack. I can't believe my pops is a goddamned crack head."

"Don't disrespect me like that. I'm still your daddy."

"Nigga, you ain't my fuckin' daddy. My pops wouldn't be this fuckin' weak minded."

J.C. took a deep breath then said, "We've all made mistakes before. Nobody is perfect, Tommy."

"I've never smoked a joint. Hell, you was the one that always told me to stay away from drugs. You were the one who told me that people who did drugs were weak."

J.C. covered his face. He was ashamed. Seconds went by and neither said anything. Finally, J.C. said, "I know I did."

"What happened?"

"I was with a woman, and she was using. I was feeling kind of fucked up because I'd lost some money in a botched real estate investment and she told me that that shit would make me feel better."

"What shit?" Tommy asked. He wanted to be sure he knew what his pops was talking about. He wanted details. He wanted the facts.

"You know""crack."

"Okay. How did it make you feel?"

"The first time I took it, I tell you the truth, nothing could beat this feeling; not even sex."

Tommy shook his head. "You're pathetic."

J.C.'s face became solemn. "It's like that, Tommy. Addicts chase the feeling of the first hit."

"You're an addict?"

"Yeah."

"So, you were so weak for a bitch that she convinced you to spend all your money on crack?"

"No, Tommy. I was depressed."

"You were weak as hell"¦you are weak as hell."

"I need your help, son."

"How the fuck am I supposed to help you?"

J.C. grabbed his son's hand then looked him in the eye. "I want you to help me get off this shit."

"You want to go to twelve steps?"

"Anything. I just want you to be there for me."

"I love you, Pops."

J.C. embraced his son then whispered, "Son, I'm sorry I let you down."

Tommy held J.C. tightly. "It's okay. We're going to make it."

17

Angie sat in the living room watching "Grey's Anatomy." Tommy walked right by her without saying a word. She paused the TiVo player using the remote control and looked in his direction. "So, you're not speaking?"

"I ain't got nothing to say." He walked into the bedroom. Angie sucked her teeth and unpaused her show.

Tommy was tired. Today had been a very eventful day for him. He needed someone to talk to, but, more than anything, he needed some rest. He kicked off his Nikes and lay in the bed with his shorts on. Angie would bitch, but he could care less about what she thought. He picked up his Blackberry and emailed Summer.

> Dear Summer,
> I hope your day was better than mine. I really needed you today. Me and Angie had it out today. She's not like you Summer and I don't know how I can truly say that I love her because today she really proved that she doesn't love me. But

that story's a long one that I don't have time to explain. My real problem is I found out today that my pops is smoking crack. I tell you that shit crushed me like you wouldn't believe. I straight up found the crack pipe in his room. When I first asked him about it, he denied it, but then he later admitted that he was smoking. I hope you don't ever go through no shit like that with either of your parents. I needed you more than anything today but I didn't want to bother you with my problems. I knew you would understand. Angie wouldn't. She's not like us. She ain't from the hood. So I didn't tell her. I hope you have a good night or if you read this in the morning, have a great morning.

Peace.

Tommy

Sent via Sprint PCS Blackberry

Q and Country were on the balcony of Q's condo smoking a blunt when Q brandished a chrome 9mm. "I swear to you, Country, that nigga has to go." Q inhaled the blunt and cocked the hammer of the gun. "You see, that's the difference between me and a lot of other getting-money niggas. You see, I'm real. I don't play the fuckin' radio. I will kill Tommy's punk ass."

"What the fuck you talking about?"

"That nigga ratted," Q said. His eyes were red from the weed smoke.

Country took the blunt from Q. "You ain't got no proof that Tommy set Squirt up."

"Squirt believes it in his heart that Tommy had something to do with it."

Country coughed some, then took another drag and finally passed the blunt to Q. "I think you need to do some research first."

"Nigga, you were the one questioning me about Tommy. Have you forgot that?"

"Yeah, but none of us has proof that Squirt was set up. I mean, why would Tommy set him up?"

"I don't know."

"Exactly."

Q tucked the gun back into his waistband then pulled out a condom. "This is how I'ma get him."

"You gonna fuck him?" Country laughed.

"No. I'ma fuck his bitch, with her fine ass." He then put the condom back into his pocket and sucked up the rest of the blunt.

Quentin seemed to be a nice guy. Though Summer didn't know much about him, she decided to meet him for lunch. She wanted to meet in a public place although it was risky since she knew she could possibly be seen by Tommy; but hey, they weren't an item. She and Q met at Fuel Pizza, downtown. Q was dressed in shorts, Timberland boots, and a wife beater. A humongous diamond glistened in his left ear. He and Summer sat at a booth in the back of the restaurant. Q looked damn good. Summer thought so herself, and she occasionally looked at the Superman symbol tattooed on his arm. Damn he had a nice body.

Q smiled again, and this time Summer quivered a little. Q had his elbows on the table, and she usually didn't like that, but she liked that roughness about him because she knew he could be gentle. He had warm eyes.

"Are you hungry?" she asked.

"No. Actually, I just wanted to see you."

"Well, I'm hungry." She smiled. "I know you're used to a lot of girls being cute and not eating, but, hell, I'm hungry."

Q laughed. "Knock yourself out. I just don't like pizza. Cheese fucks with my stomach and I don't eat meat."

Summer stood. Her jeans were gripping her ass. She hadn't planned on wearing tight jeans, but she was glad she did. Now she would sashay to the counter and watch from the corner of her eye. Her heels clacked as she walked away. She looked long, lean, and sexy. The yoga was paying off. She had the attention of every man in the pizza parlor. She glanced at Q and his eyes were glued to her ass.

"A slice of cheese and a bottle of water," she said to Kevin, noticing the name tag on the teenager behind the counter.

The boy put the pizza in the oven and handed her the water. "Did you need a cup?"

"No, I'm fine."

"That's for damn sure," Q said as he walked up behind her and pulled her hair. She felt like a high school girl. She blushed. "You like pulling on hair, huh?"

He licked his lips. "My specialty."

Kevin handed her the pizza and she and Q walked back to the booth. He sat beside her.

She bit into the slice. The cheese was like elastic as she drew the slice away from her mouth. She'd gotten cheese all over her face. As she licked it off, Q said, "Damn."

She laughed. "What?"

"Nothing. Just thinking. I bet you can do wonders with your tongue, that's all."

She busted out laughing then sat the pizza back on the paper plate. "Quentin, you are too much."

He looked in her eyes. "Listen, Summer. I been thinking about you since the day I met you, and I can't get you off my mind."

"What have you been thinking about, Q?"

"Nothing. Just that I wouldn't mind being with a girl like you."

She opened her water. "That's bullshit, Q. You want to fuck me."

Q looked the other way and didn't respond.

"That's exactly what I'm talking about, Quentin. You want to fuck me. Why don't you just go ahead and admit it?"

He shrugged and smiled. He looked very boyish at that moment and she liked that.

Finally, he said, "I ain't gonna lie. I think you fly as hell, but I really just wanted to feel you out."

She put his hand on her thigh right below her private parts, and a few seconds later he tried to feel her pussy. She moved his hands.

"What's wrong?"

"I was just seeing how far you would go." She laughed. "Niggas are easy to predict. All you want is some pussy, Q. Why don't you just admit it?"

He laughed then said, "You called me Q."

She bit down on her pizza. "I did, didn't I?"

"Yeah. It's okay though, because all my friends call me Q. I don't like that Quentin shit, anyway."

Her eyes lit up. "Quentin is the nice guy, and Q is the nigga."

"You funny."

She sat the pizza down and looked him in his eyes. "Q just wants to fuck. Quentin will treat me with respect. Q can be a womanizer. Quentin has respect for his mother and his sister."

Q looked confused. "You think you know me, shorty?"

"I don't know, but I'm just hoping there's some good in everybody."

He licked his lips again. For a few moments she imagined him between her legs, stroking her clit with his tongue. Damn, she wanted to fuck Q and not Quentin. She wanted it rough at that moment and Q seemed like he could handle the job.

"So what we doing after the pizza, shorty?"

She looked at her watch. It was only 1:00 p.m. "I have a client."

He looked startled. "What do you mean you have a client?"

"I do hair."

"What? You work in a salon or something?"

"No. I do natural hair and braids"¦twists. You know?"

"Okay. I feel you. Getting your hustle on, huh?" He laughed. Then he said, "Didn't you pull up in that red Benz?"

"Yeah." She drank some tea. "I know what you're about to say."

He grinned a toothy smile and it made her heart beat faster. "What am I about to say?"

"Probably wondering how in the hell can I afford a car like that?"

"You guessed it."

"It was a gift from a guy friend."

Q knew Tommy had probably given her the car but he would play dumb. "What you got""a sugar daddy?"

She smacked his arm with an open hand. "What, you think I'm a ho or something?"

"No, I'm just saying who the hell gives a chick a Benz except a sugar daddy or a hustler?"

"Let me change the subject, because I'm getting upset."

Q grabbed her hand and caressed it while making direct eye contact. "Listen. I'm sorry, shorty. I could care less about the car." He still caressed her hand and made a point to look into her eyes.

She yanked her hand back from him and lowered her voice. "Quentin, what do you want?"

"Nothing. I just wanna have a good time with you, that's all."

"I'm not that easy."

He wanted to ask her what she meant, but he didn't say anything.

"If you're here for pussy, it ain't that easy."

He smiled like she had read his mind. "What you like? I mean, I know you like nice things. How can I romance you?"

"Well, if you have to ask, obviously you don't know anything about romance."

Q smirked. "You don't know me. I know how to treat a lady, but the key word is lady."

"I'm one."

"Yes the fuck you are," Q said as he looked her up and down until his eyes landed on her thigh. He was amazed at her curvy figure.

"Q, I really just like simple things, like attention. That's how you can get me."

"That's it?"

"I'm not a gold digger."

He peered through the window, eyeing the Benz. He knew Tommy was fat and insecure. There was no way in the world Tommy would believe he got her just by being nice. Q looked her up and down again. Tommy had paid for her alright.

"I didn't say you was a gold digger."

"Write me a letter. That's how you can get me. Write me a heartfelt letter. I mean, share your feelings with me."

"A letter? How bout an email or a message from my Sidekick?"

She frowned. "I want a letter""that's more personal."

He looked confused. "Do people even write letters anymore?"

The goons pulled along side Tommy in a dark color SUV.

Always being conscious of his surroundings, especially at night, he looked to his left. A biracial man in the backseat of the SUV looked over and laughed at him, then blew a cloud of smoke out the window. Another man on the passenger side held a blunt to his mouth. Tommy kept his eyes on the men, from his side view mirror, while watching the light. Finally, the light turned green and Tommy quickly drove off, only to be caught by the next traffic light.

The SUV was just seconds behind him. This time when they pulled beside him, Tommy heard somebody yell from the car, "Snitch ass nigga!"

He looked over at the SUV, focusing on the gun that one of the men had pointed at him.

Tommy sped off""running the light.

He heard shots being fired.

Tommy crossed the medium in his Range Rover, turning down a side street and sped off, losing sight of the SUV.

He drove behind a building and called Angie. She answered on the fourth ring. "Tommy what the hell do you want calling at this time of night?"

"Somebody was just shooting at me!"

"What?"

He reclined his seat with the phone up to his ear and his heart pounding hard. "Yeah! Baby, somebody wants me dead!"

She sighed, not saying a word but he knew her; knew what she was thinking. He didn't really want to bother her with his problems but he had to tell somebody.

"Tommy, calm down. Where are you? Are you okay?"

"Yeah, I'm fine." He glanced over his shoulder. He thought he'd heard something; thought the goons were coming around the corner, although he'd hoped not.

"Tommy come home."

"I'm on my way." He inched out from behind the building, saw it was clear and pushed the pedal to the floor.

18

When Tommy and Angie walked into Dream's office, she looked very concerned. Dream had a blue stress ball in her hand that she was squeezing hard. She got right to the point, looking Tommy in his face. "A fed agent showed up here last night asking questions about you."

"What? Asking questions about me?" Tommy looked at Angie whose mouth was now wide open. "I haven't done anything."

Dream stood and paced without looking at them. She opened her blinds and peered out into the parking lot. It was empty except for two cars. No unmarked in sight. "Tommy, it was the DEA."

"I'm out of the drug business."

"Listen, Tommy, I'm not accusing you of anything. I'm just giving you a heads up."

"Yeah, but why would they be asking about me?"

"Maybe it's your associates. I don't know, Tommy."

"Why did they come here, of all places?"

"I think he knows that you volunteer here with me."

"Sounds like they are watching you," Angie said. "They probably watch my house too."

"Shut the fuck up. All you can think about is your house."

"Well, you say you ain't selling drugs. What you worried about?"

"Agent Mark Pratt. Does the name sound familiar?" Dream asked.

"Pratt, yeah," Tommy said and looked away. "I know him."

Angie looked at Tommy and rolled her eyes.

"I don't sell dope," Tommy said.

"Why else would they be fuckin' with you?" Angie said.

"You don't understand," Dream said before slinging the ball across the room. "Pratt is overzealous. He likes locking black men up."

"Pratt is a white man, huh?"

"No, he's black," Dream and Tommy said at the same time.

"Damn," Angie said.

"The man is just that serious. He just fucks with you and fucks with you until he gets something on you."

Dream was now playing with her hair, thinking of Pratt and the visit""how he tried to make small talk with her; how he tried to get information about Tommy. She looked Tommy directly in his eyes and said, "Tommy, whatever you're doing, stop it."

"I'm not selling coke. That game is so over."

"Tommy, why did he come asking about you?"

"I don't know," Tommy said.

"Keep ya nose clean, Tommy. I like you. You're good," she said, and then she sat behind her desk again. "That's the only reason I'm telling you about this, because you're not doing anything you're not supposed to be doing. Right?"

"That's right," Tommy said. He wasn't selling drugs. Why in the hell was Pratt asking about him? He thought about Q's boy, Squirt. Maybe he had something to do with this.

"Feds? What the fuck, nigga. You ain't making no real money. Why in the hell would they be looking for you?" Ditty was breaking up buds on a CD cover; regular weed. He'd wanted some purple haze but wasn't able to locate any. His regular supplier didn't have any.

"I don't know. Who the fuck knows?"

"Q's boy. Maybe he told them something about you?" Ditty said, now pouring the weed in a Dutch Master cigar.

"Tell them what? That I sold him a car?"

Licking the blunt and sealing it, Ditty continued. "You never know, man. Those niggas could have said that you traded them cars for drugs. You never know what kind of shit motherfuckers come up with when they're under pressure."

"But they are saying I told."

"That's a cover up, man. Those niggas know you didn't tell."

"Why did they shoot at me, then?"

Ditty lit the blunt. "No. The question is why the fuck didn't we shoot back?"

"And on top of that, my girl is tripping, man. She thinks I'm hustling"|mean, selling drugs again," Tommy said.

Ditty blew out a huge cloud of smoke almost in Tommy's face.

Tommy fanned the smoke before standing. He paced nervously. "I don't know what to do."

"Do what the fuck you been doing. I mean, bro', we got a sweet hustle, dude. We ain't selling no fuckin' dope. I don't give a damn if they do think we are. I don't give a fuck if they following us. They will see we legit."

"Legit? What the fuck you mean we legit? Selling stolen cars ain't legit."

Ditty inhaled the weed again, coughed hard then pounded himself on the chest. "I mean we legit compared to other motherfuckers and compared to the shit we used to do. Nobody is looking for car salesmen. We don't steal the cars, we just sell them."

"Salesmen, huh?"

Ditty stood. His eyes were now red and the weed had turned him into a philosopher. Tommy had seen him like this before. Right now, Ditty was an expert on every subject matter. He could ask him about the rising gas prices, why Tiger Woods was the best golfer, who killed Malcolm X"¦ he would know the answer to anything, now, and he'd give him a conspiracy theory to go along with his answers.

"But, Ditty, it's the same guy that busted me the last time."

"Fuck him," Ditty said. He stubbed the blunt out. "You know why nothing is going to happen?"

Tommy shook his head yes, but he knew Ditty was going to tell him anyway.

When Summer opened the letter, she was thrilled. Quentin had actually written her.

Dear Summer,

I have to admit this letter writing stuff ain't me. I mean, I'm Q. Niggas respect me because I'm hardcore, but hey, nobody has to know that I have a soft spot sometimes. But I also have to admit I've never met a chick like you. I mean, I think it's just amazing how we met that day. I didn't even want to go out, but you know when God wants something to happen it happens and I think that me meeting you was God's work. I think you are my soul mate, Summer. I know you are probably saying how ridiculous is that, but really I haven't met a chick like you in a while, a very long time. You are life Summer, and I am very glad we connected. I kind of thought this whole idea was funny, I mean nobody has ever had me to write a letter before, I mean besides, you know, the elementary school Do-you-love-me-yes-or-no letters, but I guess you didn't let the Timberlands and the do-rag fool you. But hopefully after this letter you will see that Q has brains. Not much on long letters, but I have poured out my heart.

Your Boy,

Q

Summer smiled then folded the letter back into the envelope. Quentin had sense after all. She knew he did most of what those hardcore thugs did; they just all pretended to be tougher than what they really were. She decided to call him. He picked up on the first ring.

"You."

"Got your letter, Quentin."

"Come on, shorty. Can you chill with that Quentin stuff?"

"Why you try to act so tough?"

"Cuz where I'm from the weak get devoured."

"Really," she said as she walked to the arm of the sofa.

"So what's going on tonight?"

"Not much. Just watching TV"¦some old episodes of "'Fame.'"

"What you know about "'Fame'? You too young for that."

"What do you know about "'Fame' is the question.?

"How old do you think I am, Q?"

A long pause on the phone. She knew he was thinking, probably not wanting to make the wrong guess. "I think maybe 27."

"Good guess."

"Me too."

"I was born in '80," Summer said.

"Yeah? What month? June, July"¦?"

"How did you guess?"

"Duh"¦your name is Summer."

She laughed. "So, Q, you want to come watch "'Fame' with me?"

"Hell yeah."

"I live by the Verizon Amphitheater."

"The University area, right? I can be there in twenty minutes."

19

When Summer opened the door, she was looking more fascinating than ever. She was wearing skinny jeans that gripped her thighs and made her ass look perfect, and heels that made her look even more long and lean. Q's dick became semi-erect. He wanted to peel those jeans off her right at that moment. He looked at her feet and imagined sucking those cute little toes. He knew he could make her love him. When the show started, Summer sang along. She stood, kicked off her shoes and yelled "Fame! I'm gonna live forever"!"

She spun around like a ballerina.

"I always wanted to be a dancer but was never good at it," she said.

Q grabbed her hand and spun her around.

Summer giggled then said, "What are you doing?"

"Dancing."

"Nigga, this is ballroom dancing you are doing. There is a difference."

"What were you doing?" he asked. A nigga like Q didn't know the difference, nor did he care. He never danced. He had a little two step that he would do at parties. He had done this for years, but dancing was for homos and girls. He was a gangster, and what he wanted to do was unbutton that blouse because those nipples were erect and her body language said she wanted him to do that.

She looked into his eyes briefly then turned away. "Q, what would your friends say if they knew you were here with me watching "'Fame' and dancing?"

"I don't know, nor do I give a fuck." Q smiled as she put her arm around his waist, and they both took a seat on the sofa together. She turned to Q and said, "Name one character on this show."

He shrugged. "I don't know" the gay dude with the braids."

She laughed. "Q, you don't really watch this do you?"

"No. I mean, I've seen it a couple of times, but no, I am not a fan."

"Why did you lie?"

"I don't know. I wanted to see you." He rubbed her feet.

"Damn that feels good, baby. Keep doing it."

He put his hand on her inner thigh and she pushed it away. Seconds later it was there again. She moaned then pushed it away. He turned and pushed his tongue down her throat. She grabbed the remote control and paused the TV; she then unbuttoned her blouse. He removed her bra as he kicked off his Jordans. He kissed her neck and she removed her jeans. She was now wet. She led his hand to her ass.

"Yeah, baby. Grip that ass." His hands were big enough to hold her whole ass in his palms. Her hot spot.

When Q pulled his T-shirt over his head, he took off his chain and watch. His dick peeked through his boxers. Summer put her hands on it then pulled his shorts down. She massaged it.

He didn't want head. He wanted to put it inside her. He wanted to see that round ass from behind; her making faces while he pulled her hair. He stopped her from massaging his dick and kissed her on her neck. She placed his hand on her ass again.

"Put it inside me."

He pushed her onto the sofa, spread her legs and entered. She moaned. He was gentle and she liked that because he was big; much bigger than Tommy.

"Tell me what you like," he requested.

"Just grab my leg." She lifted it for him and he held it.

"Baby this pussy is so wet."

"You like it?"

A stupid question that came up sometimes. What nigga didn't like pussy unless he, of course, liked dick. And then, if he liked dick, this question would never come up.

Q continued to stroke while gripping her ass. She rubbed his chest.

"Turn over on your side," he said.

When she did, he pulled her hair. "Smack my ass," she said. She was a freak with no inhibitions.

"Pull my hair harder."

He wrapped her hair around the palm of his hand and kept pulling. She made faces and it seemed to be arousing her. He kept thrusting. Finally, he flipped her over onto her stomach to enter her doggy style.

"How does it feel, baby?" he asked.

There were tears in her eyes now. Why did men have to ask so many damn stupid questions at the wrong time?

"Right there. Keep going. Keep going. Don't move," she said.

He had her spot; she didn't want him to mess it up. He kept thrusting, trying to shift, and when he did, she lay on her back and demanded it missionary style.

He entered again, gripping her ass and thrusting hard until she came hard.

He pulled out. She bounced from the sofa and disappeared into the bathroom. She came back with a wet wash cloth. She wiped him off and began to suck his balls. She said she felt bad because he hadn't cum. His head fell back and he couldn't believe she was this freaky.

The smacking sound drove him crazy. He ran his fingers through her hair, trying his best to cum, but he could never come from oral.

Five minutes later she looked up and asked, "What's wrong?"

"Oh, nothing. I just don't like this. I like the real thing."

She stood and smiled then placed his hand on her ass again and his dick became erect again. She fell back on the sofa and he entered her.

The pussy was so wet and her screaming was so intense. He came inside her. She held him tight again, and then she trembled. More tears came down her face.

He got up smiling. He looked at her sexy ass again, wanting more sex, but he knew it would be at least fifteen minutes before he would be erect again. Her clock read 8:45. He needed to meet Country in an hour. He asked where her bathroom was so he could shower.

She said, "Me first." Then disappeared down the hallway.

When Q came out of the shower, Summer was sitting on the sofa with glasses on watching "Fame." She winked at him when he entered the room. "I fixed you a sandwich."

"What kind?" he asked.

"Tuna."

He laughed. "I must have been good."

"You were okay. I've had better."

Picking up his Jordans he said, "Right."

Fatboy damn sure couldn't put it down. So he knew she couldn't be talking about him.

She stood from the sofa and walked toward him. She put her arms around him and laid her head on his chest.

His heart was pulsating. He hugged her. His body was so warm she could stay in his arms forever. She had just met him though, and she'd never felt like this about someone so quickly.

When she released him he put his boxers back on; then the jeans, the Jordans, and finally the T-shirt. He noticed she was still looking at him.

"What's wrong?"

"Are you coming back?"

"What about your boyfriend?"

"Let me worry about that."

He looked at his watch then back at her. She was smiling.

The look on her face said, Stay here and fuck my brains out. He wanted to do just that, but he had business to tend to""important business.

"Baby I will be back tomorrow, I promise."

She put her arms around him again. He kissed her forehead.

"What the fuck do you mean he got away?" Q said to Mario, the tallest of the three goons.

Mario was a tall nigga with a bucked gold tooth and a bald head. "I don't know how he got away. I mean, I didn't shoot. I was driving."

Q stepped up to Mario and grabbed his white shirt, ripping it, then pushed the man backward. "Motherfucker. You were driving the car. You are the very reason the nigga got away. You should have caught him!"

Mario turned to Puff, a short man with braids and bubble lips. He was the shooter.

Puff trembled and fumbled trying to light a cigarette. "I'ma get him, Q. Don't worry."

Q backhanded Puff and the cigarette flew from his hand. Puff then rushed Q. Country brandished a chrome Taurus 9mm and cocked the hammer. "Motherfuckers. Don't even try it."

Puff stopped in his tracks. Q smacked him again and again, then he took the gun from Country and bashed Puff's head. Blood oozed from his forehead. Q then picked up some dirt from the ground and smeared it on the open sore. "Motherfucker, I will kill yo bitch ass."

Puff held his head, attempting to walk away, but Q then kicked him as hard as he could in the side of the ribs. "I paid y'all bitch asses three grand to take this man out, and you mean to tell me he's still walking around here?"

Corey, the third man, a biracial with a ponytail and the smartest of the three, said, "Don't worry, Q. We gonna take him out."

Q grimaced. "If you don't take him out, I'ma get my money back and then I'ma have somebody fuck y'all bitch-asses up."

Corey pulled out three stacks of $100 bills and showed them

to Q. "I still got the money. I am not spending it until the job is done."

Puff still held his head, staring at Q, but he was afraid to say anything. It wasn't fair that he got pistol whipped and had to accept it. Mario got the balls to ask Q a question that he'd been wanting to ask ever since they had agreed to take the job. "Who did big boy rat on?"

"None of your fuckin' business."

Q wasn't about to tell these idiots anything. The less they knew, the better.

Corey looked at Mario. "Why do you wanna know that anyway?"

Country said, "Yeah, nigga. Mind your fuckin' business."

Mario had wanted to ask something else but was afraid he would be the next to get the Taurus 9mm against his bald head. That was not a good thought to him.

The goons got into the SUV and drove off.

J.C.'s phone rang. He started not to answer it, thinking it was a bill collector again, but he recognized the number. Shantell.

He answered. "Hello."

"Daddy, have you forgotten you were supposed to help me with rent today?"

J.C. hadn't forgotten. The truth was he didn't have the money. He had gone through all of what he had gotten from the bank. He didn't know how he would pay his mortgage.

"Daddy? Did you hear me?"

"Stop calling me Daddy. That shit makes me feel older than I already feel."

"Sorry, honey bun," she said.

J.C. stood and walked over to his dresser drawer to look for money. There were two $20 bills and a five and three ones. Not enough to pay Shantell's $1,100 rent""nowhere near that amount. And it was damn sure not enough to pay his $1,400 mortgage. "I will have the money tomorrow."

"But today is the fifth, honey."

"I don't have it yet."

"I have a surprise for you. I'm wearing that hot pink skirt and that lip gloss that you like so much."

J.C.'s dick rose a little. Thinking about Shantell's lips around his dick made him excited; made him want to see her. He thought about her lying across his bed in a pink thong. He wanted to see her, but he didn't have the money that he knew she wanted. He uttered, "Damn."

"What's wrong?"

"Nothing. I was just wondering when can I see you?"

"I just told you that I was wearing your favorite outfit, Daddy, and that lip gloss. And you know that I know how to work my tongue ring."

"Come over in an hour," he said.

"Your house?"

"Yeah."

"What about your son?"

"Don't worry about him. He's not coming over."

"I will be there soon, Daddy."

He hated the word Daddy, though he was old enough to be her granddaddy and technically, he was her sugar daddy. Maybe that's why he hated the word so much.

20

J.C. climbed into the attic moving old shoes and boxes out of his way as he looked around in the dark. Where the hell is the safe, chest, shoebox, or whatever the money is in, he thought. He stumbled upon some photo albums. He opened them""a picture of Tommy, him, and Tommy's mother Natalie at the lake when Tommy was in the first grade. J.C. remembered that day well. He had bought Tommy his first fishing pole. Tommy had been a happy kid ever since he was a baby. He was easygoing. Although J.C. wasn't his biological father, he'd been around since Tommy was a few months old. Tommy was his son.

He quickly closed the photo album. He didn't want to think about his deceased wife. He didn't want to think of her looking down on him. She had always despised drugs. He moved a suitcase out of his way and threw a box of coats down from the attic. Where the fuck is the money?

He knew Tommy had money there, but he didn't know how much. He would take a few thousand then replace it. He had a watch he could sell and make at least five grand. That would easily cover money that he would take.

Underneath two bags of shoes, he found a Nike shoebox with bundles of cash in it. He figured it had to be at least $150,000. Tommy always had a knack for making that money. J.C. took $4,000 from the stash.

When J.C. opened the door, Shantell didn't have the dress on that she'd promised, but she was looking phenomenal. Her jeans gripped her ass and thighs, and her heels were at least five inches. J.C. imagined himself fucking her while she wore nothing but the heels.

She licked her lips. The pink lip gloss was fresh and he had gotten a glimpse of her tongue ring.

"What happened to the dress?"

She laughed and moved closer with her hair flowing and the smell of Escada's Sunset Heat perfume lingering in the air. He knew that smell. It was what she always wore for him when she tried to get money from him. It drove him wild. He couldn't take his eyes off of her lips. He remembered where his money had gone so fast, and tonight it would be $200 for head and $900 for Shantell's rent. Damn, he cursed himself. But he couldn't resist.

"I can't wear that every time, Daddy." She was now face to face with him. "Don't you think I'm sexy?"

Her hands slid down J.C's shirt to rub his belly.

He sat down on the sofa. His hand was now on her ass, and he began rubbing it.

Her ass cheeks were perfectly round, like two small basketballs. He slid his hands into the back of her jeans, trying to find her thong.

She whispered, "I ain't got no panties on."

Shantell dropped to her knees, unbuttoned his pants and then unzipped them. His dick was out, still limp though, until she rubbed it on her lip gloss and put his balls in her mouth.

"Yeah," he said, looking up at the ceiling. Sure this was going to cost him, but the scent of the Sunset Heat smelled so damn good.

They met at the car wash. Scooter's Escalade looked a lot different than before. It was sitting on 26-inch rims. When he pulled up, he was playing Jay-Z's "Blueprint" album. Scooter jumped out the Escalade leaving it running; pulled out his Newports and gave one to Ditty. "Tommy, what's on your mind?" Scooter asked.

"Problems."

"I'm the problem solver," Scooter said, blowing smoke rings.

"Some niggas tried to kill me a few days ago."

"What?" Scooter said.

Tommy was silent. Jay-Z and Eminem traded verses on "Renegade" in the background.

"Who tried to kill you?"

"Niggas. I really don't know."

Ditty puffed his cigarette. "We think it's a nigga named Q, from Wilmore."

"I know that faggot-ass nigga. He supposedly getting money"|hustling motherfucker, right?"

"Yeah," Tommy said.

Scooter turned his ignition off. The music faded. His face was now very serious.

"Tommy, you don't fuck with nobody. Why these niggas want to fuck with you?"

It didn't make sense. Tommy was very likable. Never crossed anybody. Not a bad ass at all.

"He think I set his boy up."

Scooter raised his eyebrow. "But you don't hustle"|I mean"|sell dope, do you?"

"Hell no."

"Then how the fuck did you set his man up?" Scooter puffed his cigarette then flicked it to the pavement.

"He saying I sold his boy a car and the police busted him. Basically saying that I told the police to look out for the car."

"Bullshit," Scooter said. "Any motherfucker that knows you know you ain't do no shit like that."

"Exactly," Ditty said.

Scooter looked directly into Tommy's eyes. "So, how ya wanna handle it?"

"I say find out where that nigga's mama live and send some shots through her house," Ditty said.

"Naw" we have to be smart," Tommy said.

"What do you have in mind?" Scooter asked.

Tommy didn't respond immediately. Q needed to be taught a lesson, but Tommy didn't want to go back to prison. Pratt was watching.

"Do you have a trigger man?"

"Hell yeah. The best."

"I want to find out who shot at me. Follow them, and they will take us to where Q lays his head. I really don't want to get into shooting in nobody's mama's house."

Putting an innocent person in harm's way was just not the right way to do things.

"I got the perfect trigger man""one-man operation. He will find out who done this to you, Tommy."

"Who is it?"

"My nigga, J-Black, from North Charlotte."

"J-J-J- Black?" Tommy said.

"Yeah. What? You know him?"

"Kind of."

J-Black had robbed Tommy several years ago, and though he knew about it, he didn't give J-Black up when the feds had busted him.

"Did he rob you before?" Scooter asked.

"Yeah," Tommy said. But what he didn't say was J-Black had robbed him three times. Even tied his ex-girlfriend up and fucked her in front of Tommy. J-Black had also killed one of Tommy's best friends, Twin.

"Don't worry. I got him. I can handle him. As long as he's getting paid, everything will be okay," Scooter said. He pulled another Newport from the pack.

"Give me one of those," Tommy said.

"But you don't smoke."

"I know," Tommy said, then grabbed a lighter from Ditty.

21

Tonya was making another daiquiri""her third. After pouring it into the wine glass, she was walking back into Summer's living room when Summer said, "I fucked Q."

Tonya almost spilled her drink. "You did what?"

"Q. You remember Q, the guy I met at the martini bar."

Tonya sat on the sofa smiling and sipped her drink. "I didn't know y'all were kicking it."

They really weren't kicking it technically. They had gone out a couple of times. She had called him and he had call her and written her a letter, but they weren't kicking it. Summer didn't know how to define their relationship.

"We're not."

"What happened?" Tonya asked, wanting to know all the details.

Summer blushed but didn't say anything.

"Was he big?"

Summer didn't know how to answer that one. Didn't really want to answer that one. She knew from past experiences that if a man could fuck good, some women would make it their business to fuck your man.

"Come on Summer, what happened?" Tonya asked, leaning forward.

"He took me out."

Smiling, then swallowing another sip from her glass, Tonya asked, "Where did y'all go?"

"Fuel Pizza."

"Wait a minute. A nigga buys you pizza and you give him the goods?"

Summer frowned. Everything was always about money with Tonya; always about what you could get out of a man.

Tonya laughed. "Girl, please tell me you didn't give that ass up for a meat lover's pizza."

"No, we fucked because I wanted to fuck."

"But what can Q offer?"

"I don't know what he can offer, or what he will offer, but I like him."

"What about Tommy?"

"Tommy has a live-in."

"But you like him."

Summer didn't say anything. She didn't want to think about Tommy. Though Tommy had a live-in, Summer loved him and would never want to hurt him.

"So you say Q has a big dick?"

"I didn't say that," Summer said.

"His dick is small?"

"No."

"Can he fuck?"

Summer blushed again, but not wanting to say how Q wore her pussy out, she said, "He's good."

"You like him don't you?"

"Yeah."

Tonya put her glass down. "But what about Tommy?"

Mark Pratt walked into Special Agent-in-Charge Doug Sanders' office carrying Tommy Dupree's folder.

Sanders was in his swivel chair on the phone. When he was done with his conversation he motioned for Pratt to take a seat. "What's on your mind?"

"Tommy Dupree."

Sanders frowned. Dupree's name did not ring a bell.

"I took him down a few years ago for Ecstasy."

"Oh yeah?"

"Yeah. He got five years."

"Cooperated?"

"No, not really. Just gave information about an agent that slept with him."

"Oh yeah. I remember this one."

"Yeah, I think he's doing dirt again."

"What?"

"Yeah."

"What you think he's doing?" Sanders' eyes were curious. He spun in the swivel chair with a blue ballpoint pen in his mouth.

"I don't know."

"What makes you think he's doing dirt?"

"The state busted a guy with nine ounces."

"He ratted on Dupree, huh?"

"No. He thinks Dupree ratted on him."

"This is better than "'The Wire'," Sanders said.

"Yeah. I know."

"But you were saying that he thinks Dupree ratted on him?"

"Yeah."

"Why does he think that?"

"I don't know."

"So what's up with Dupree nowadays?"

"Counseling kids" trying to act like he's straight, but I know better." Mark opened the folder and looked at Tommy's picture.

"Why do you think he's doing something wrong?"

"Followed him one day."

"And?"

"Observed what looked like a drug exchange between him and two white boys."

"White kids?"

Sanders said it as if he wasn't white himself. Had told Pratt before he was Irish and not white. He was only white when it mattered.

"Yeah. They gave him an Escalade and he'd given them a bag of money."

Sanders flicked the pen. "Are you sure it was a drug deal?"

"No."

"Pratt, I want you to leave this alone. We have other shit to worry about."

"Leave it alone? I'm not understanding?"

"Just leave it alone."

Pratt stood and was about to walk out the office when he turned to Sanders. "Do you want me to leave it alone because I think his connect is white?"

Squirt was on his second set of twenty-five push ups, sweating; he wiped his eyes with his shirt when the deputy walked in and announced mail call.

"Jerome Miller." He rushed the Deputy, anxious to read his mail. It was the only thing that got him through the day""the thing he looked forward to the most. The letter smelled like perfume. Squirt sniffed the letter and another inmate yelled. "Can I sleep with that envelope, shorty?"

"Hell fuckin' no," Squirt said, disappearing into his cell. He hopped onto his bunk and tore into the letter.

Squirt,

The baby's getting bigger everyday. He picked up your picture the other day and smiled. I know he wants to know where his daddy is. Q paid the phone bill and he sent someone over here to buy some Pampers and milk, but I need some help with the rent. I really don't want to ask Q because he's done so much and I don't want to go back to Mama's house. You know how she is. I was over there the other day and you know my stupid-ass sister Tyeisha said some slick shit like you ain't gonna ever be shit but a drug dealer. I cussed her ass out, but I cried. Baby, I'm trying to be strong for you, but this shit is hard. I cry all the time when you ain't here to hold me. You know how you be gripping my ass when we sleep"¦you know I miss that so much. But, baby, you have to get out of there. I'm not telling you to tell on Q because he helps out so much. I'm just trippin' baby. Do your time like a man. Be a soldier for mommy. You know I ain't fuckin' with nobody, so don't even worry about that shit. This pussy is tight for you baby. I love you and here is a picture of the baby.

Love always,

Tia

Squirt closed his eyes and took a deep breath.

Jessie, his cell mate, walked into the room. "Stay strong, young brother."

Squirt opened his eyes, smiled then handed Jessie a picture of his son. "This is my son, Jaylen."

"He's a cute little fella. You gotta get back out there to him."

"I know. I figure if I can get three years I will be okay."

Jessie handed him the picture and sat on the bed. "Yeah, sounds about right, if the feds don't pick the case up."

If the feds got the case he would do at least ten years. They would send him to some redneck town with a small population, or maybe Kentucky. He'd had a friend named T-Money who had done federal time, and the whole time he was down he would call Squirt complaining about the redneck correctional officers. He said they'd sent him somewhere far, where his mom could only visit him once a year. He wasn't cool with his mom, but his girl wouldn't be able to see him regularly, and his son would be almost ten when he got out. Maybe Tia would find her another man. Another man would raise his son. Damn, he hated to think about that. Didn't want to think about the feds, but he knew that was a possibility.

"You think they will pick it up?" Squirt asked.

Jessie shrugged. "Who knows? But don't die in here worrying about shit you can't control."

Jessie was right. He couldn't control his fate. He could only look forward to his

22

Tommy stood on the bridge of the Catawba River wondering what it would be like to jump. The river was one hundred feet below. He had never thought about suicide before; always considered it a sin. The old folks always said that was the one sin that God would not forgive. Tommy wanted to be in God's good graces and he wanted to see his mother again. He had always felt he would see her when he went to heaven. The water down below was shallow. There was nothing but big rocks mostly. He knew that he would die instantly. Did he want to go like that? Did he want to go at all? His life was so troubled. This fuckin' Mark Pratt was after him again, and Q and his boys thought he was a rat. He knew that this was the worst thing that he could ever be accused of. Those niggas in the SUV shooting at him thought he was a rat. One of them called him a snitch. His cell phone rang""Summer.

"What's up?"

"What you doing?"

"Nothing."

"Where are you, Tommy?"

"Why?"

"Because it's quiet. I've never called you and it was so quiet."

"I know." Tommy looked down below at the rocks. They would kill him okay, and he would be found by an old fisherman. It happened all the time.

"Tommy, are you okay?"

"Y-yeah. Why do you ask?"

"I haven't heard from you that's all."

"You miss me?"

"Why you asking me that Tommy?"

"No reason." He wondered if he were gone who would miss him. Who would care? His pops would miss him. He knew it would break his father's heart if he committed suicide. He was all J.C. had.

"Tommy, I'll talk to you later. Or just call me when you get some time."

Tommy didn't say anything. He terminated the call, walked back to his truck and drove off.

J-Black looked just like Tommy remembered, but only a few pounds heavier. J-Black was sitting on the passenger side of Scooter's car when Tommy walked up. He was grinning as Tommy approached.

"J-Black says he will find all them niggas one by one."

"He knows my work," J-Black said. "He know it very well. Ain't that right, Fatboy?"

He didn't like the tone in which J-Black spoke to him. Sure he'd robbed him a few times in the past, but this nigga was downright disrespectful. "Okay, you come to work or you want to talk about history?"

"J-Black is on our side."

"Yeah, nigga. I just want to get paid."

J-Black and Tommy's eyes met before Tommy turned to Scooter. "So how much money he want?"

"Five thousand dollars a body. I'm a pro at this," J-Black responded.

"I just want Q taken out. You know, if you kill the head, the body dies."

"Yeah, but I have to figure out how to get to Q."

"You know him?" Tommy asked.

"No, and I don't give a fuck about him. When I tell you I'ma get his bitch ass, consider it done."

"I don't have $20,000."

J-Black laughed then said, "Well, give me ten since we're old buddies."

"I'm not giving you money before the job is done."

Scooter turned to J-Black. "Half before and half when the job is done."

"I'll get started tomorrow." He smiled a wicked smile but Tommy knew that J-Black was serious. He didn't like him but he knew that he would get the job done.

The shoebox wasn't where he'd left it. Tommy searched frantically for his money. He knew it had to be there. He left it there and nobody knew where it was.

When he turned the light on, he saw the Nike shoebox under a bunch of old newspapers. He opened it and it was still full of money, but he had to count it. Something wasn't right. The money wasn't where it should have been. He knew there should have been $138,000. That is what he had previously, but after counting he discovered there was $4,000 missing.

He quickly walked into his pops' bedroom. The room smelled like feet and beer. Empty beer cans lay on the floor.

His dad was lying on the bed watching the Discovery Channel. He looked up and made eye contact with Tommy. Tommy set the box on the dresser that was right beside J.C.'s television.

An ashtray on the dresser revealed cigarette butts with lipstick on them.

"Hey, son. I didn't know you were here."

"Don't hey son me. Where the fuck is my money?" Tommy said. He scanned the room, looking for more evidence of a party""cocaine baggies or crack pipes, but he didn't see either. A tiny pink thong was in the corner of the room next to J.C's bed. Tommy walked over and picked up the panties. He held them in the air.

J.C. chuckled. He was proud of his conquest. But when he saw that Tommy was pissed, he stopped laughing.

"What the fuck are these?" Tommy said.

"They are panties. I think you know what panties are"¦don't you?"

"Buying pussy, huh?" Tommy said, shaking his head.

"So what makes you say that?"

Tommy paced, picked up the shoebox and then put it down again. "Nigga, the kind of women you date wear bloomers, not thongs."

"Your point?" J.C. asked. He was in no mood for anybody preaching to him, but he knew he had to listen to him. He had spent the money and there was really no way he could replace it.

"There was a young bitch here and my money is gone." He picked up the shoebox again. "I know exactly how much money I had, and you spent it, nigga."

"Why you talking to me like that?"

"I want my fuckin' money."

J.C. stood, not knowing what to say. He wished he could magically replace the four grand that he'd taken, but he couldn't, nor could he deny taking it.

"Where the fuck is the money?" Tommy said, holding the Nike shoebox. "I know how I left the money in the attic. Know where it was; the exact spot."

J.C. sighed as he put his hands into his pocket. "Son, I'm not going to lie to you. I took your money and I was going to put it back."

"Replace my money? You were going to replace my money, nigga? How you gonna replace my money?"

J.C. reached for Tommy, attempting to hug him, but Tommy pushed him away. "Get the fuck off me."

"I'm still your daddy."

"I don't know my daddy, nigga. You ain't nothing to me. Nothing but a fuckin' crack head."

A single tear ran down J.C.'s face. Tommy regretted what

he had said to him. He was the only father Tommy had known; had been with him for as long as he could remember, and had loved his mother more than life. He was the one who'd given the attorney the money to save his ass from his last drug case.

"Son, I have been there for you."

He had visited him in prison, taught him how to be a man and loved him unconditionally, probably more than anything. He was the only person that Tommy had.

Tommy avoided his eyes. "Why did you steal from me?"

"I needed the money."

"For what?"

"To save the house."

Tommy made eye contact with J.C. "I thought you had gotten the money from the bank; thought you'd refinanced the house."

"I did."

"And the money's gone already?"

Tommy looked up at the ceiling. There was a long silence before J.C. said, "Nobody is perfect."

"You're weak."

J.C. had had enough of Tommy's insults. "And you're weak, nigga. You're out here selling that shit again. You think I don't know what you're doing? You think I don't know what you are into?"

"I ain't selling shit."

"Put your fuckin' money in the bank then, Tommy. If you got the money legitimately, then put it in the bank. Nobody with justifiable income keeps money in a shoebox, Tommy. Do you think I'm crazy?"

Tommy sighed then looked at his father, but made no comment. The man was pathetic and weak for a piece of ass, and he was a junkie. He was someone Tommy could never respect again. Not only was he a coke head but he was a thief. He imagined the little bitch in the pink thong with maybe 5- or 6-inch heels. She was probably about 25-years-old""a high-class whore or a stripper who made the old man feel young. Maybe she gave him head. A lot of men were suckers for head. While sucking his dick, she most likely asked for the money.

She was good. She managed to juice his father out of at least a half million dollars. He could imagine her calling him, making him feel young and feeding him sob stories about not having enough money for rent, or needing money for a new car. He was game to the deception of women. He, just like every other man, had paid for companionship at one time or another. But when you blow hundreds of thousands of dollars on drugs and women, you are pathetic.

Their eyes met and held. "You could have asked," Tommy said.

J.C. dropped his head. "I was embarrassed, son."

"Well, now I'm embarrassed that I even fuckin' know you."

J.C. knew Tommy was hurting. He eased toward him, attempting to hug him.

Tommy pushed him back and J.C. fell onto the bed. Seconds later he sprang from the bed and charged Tommy, but was quickly restrained as Tommy pinned his arms down.

"Let me go," J.C. said. He continued to try to break free.

"Fuck you," Tommy said, then he raised his right hand. He wanted to break his nose but he couldn't punch his father for two reasons""he had respect for his mother and he knew if she were living she wouldn't approve of it. Also, everybody would say he was wrong for hitting J.C.; beating up an old man. But he wanted to treat him like any other nigga in the street who had stolen from him.

"Go ahead and hit me. Everything I've done for you"¦and this is the fuckin' thanks I get!"

"How the hell did you become so damn weak?" Tommy said. He then released J.C. from his grips and lowered his hand.

J.C. got up from the bed, disentangled his shirt and tidied himself up a bit. "I made a mistake, okay? Like you've never made a mistake."

"How in the hell was that a mistake? You took my motherfuckin' money!"

Neither man said anything. Tommy turned his back and was about to walk away.

"Son, I wasn't prepared for this. I have never had money before in my life. That's how I lost the money. I mean, everything was just so overwhelming. I came out of prison going from not having money to having it all, and I wasn't ready to handle it."

Tommy turned and faced his father. He was angry, but J.C. was the only person that he could somewhat trust. The only person that knew him.

"Son it won't happen again. I promise you, son."

"I know it's not going to happen again, because I ain't fuckin' with you," Tommy said as he grabbed the shoebox and exited the room.

23

The first thing Tommy noticed when Summer opened the door were the red Spandex shorts she was wearing, but he wasn't in the mood for sex.

"Tommy, how the fuck are you just going to show up at my house without calling?"

Tommy looked surprised. What the fuck was she saying? She was his lady. Nobody had ever told him when to show up at their apartment. "Do you have company?"

"No."

"Why you tripping?"

"Tommy, I don't even know where the fuck you live, but you can come over my house anytime you want? That shit ain't cool."

He chuckled. "So you want to know where I live?"

"I don't give a fuck where you live, but you gonna respect my house."

"Can I come in?"

She moved aside and he entered the apartment. She was watching "Top Model." She sat on the sofa and he sat across from her. Five minutes after sitting down his eyes were closed. When Summer saw this she said, "Tommy, are you asleep?"

He raised himself up. "No. I'm not asleep; just thinking." He closed his eyes again.

"What's wrong?"

"My pops is a crack head."

"What are you gonna do?"

Tommy sighed. He really didn't want to talk about it but he needed to talk to somebody. He needed to get it out.

Her facial expression said that she didn't understand. Maybe nobody in her immediate family had ever been on drugs.

"Tommy, you want to talk about it?"

"I mean, there is nothing to talk about. The man is a straight up crack head."

With the remote control in hand, Summer paused "Top Model" then turned it off. Tommy needed her.

"He stole from me."

"But your dad has money."

"You mean had money."

"What are you talking about?"

"The man has blown all his money on coke and young bitches."

"What?" She couldn't believe what she was hearing. She remembered Tommy telling her that his father was awarded more than two million dollars. Now he was broke? She couldn't see how, but then, poor people who are awarded that kind of money usually wind up broke again.

"Yeah, the nigga is broke," Tommy said.

"What did he steal from you?"

"He stole some money," Tommy said. "I'd left some money in the attic and he took some of it."

"Oh." She felt sorry for Tommy. He looked as if his whole world had come to an end. She moved over to his seat, sat on his lap and kissed his forehead. "I'm sorry, honey."

"Don't worry. This ain't your problem; it's mine."

"What can I do to help?"

"Nothing, really" I mean, unless you gonna rehab the nigga." Tommy laughed, not because what he said was funny, but because he wanted to keep from crying.

"You think he wants help?"

"I don't know if he wants help. I know he needs it."

She tried to kiss him again, but he dodged her lips. "What were you tripping for earlier?"

"What you mean?"

"You got all fuckin' bent out of shape when I came."

"Because you came without calling or texting me."

"I have a lot of shit on my mind. That's why. But what's the problem?"

She stood and walked away. Her ass looked marvelous in those Spandex shorts. Tommy stood and walked behind her, and when she sat on the couch he joined her. She turned the TV back on to "Top Model," trying to ignore Tommy's advances. He put his hand on her thigh, trying to feel her pussy, but she pushed him away.

He was confused. "What's wrong?"

"Nothing is wrong. I'm not in the mood for it," she said.

"Wait a minute. What's up with this attitude?"

"I don't have no attitude. I mean, Tommy, you always try to act like it's all about you."

Summer was really acting illogical. First she was trying to comfort him, then she didn't want him to touch her. He wondered what that was all about.

"Tommy, you got a life, another life with a woman who damn sure ain't me."

Tommy moved to the other side of the room. She was emotional now and he was a little worked up from earlier. He would remain calm and not let his feelings get the best of him.

"Tommy, I just didn't like you popping up like that. It's not really a problem," she said. She knew he was confused because there had never been a problem before. There had never been rules established, but she figured he should have known better, especially now since she was digging Q.

"So what the fuck is up with all these regulations?"

"No regulations, Tommy. It's just that I think you should

respect me."

"I've been disrespecting you?"

"No"¦"

"What are you talking about?"

"Nothing. Tommy, you wouldn't understand."

"You seeing somebody else or something?"

"Of course not," she said, but she wouldn't look him in the eyes.

"Okay, what's the problem?"

"You wouldn't understand." She stood and headed to the kitchen, not really wanting anything, but she had to get away. She could not and would not tell Tommy about Q. When she opened the fridge she grabbed a bottle of water then turned to meet Tommy.

"I think it's another nigga," he said, grabbing her ass. She pushed his hand away.

"Tommy, I'm not in the mood."

He frowned.

She loosened the bottle cap, took a swallow, and then made eye contact with him but didn't say anything.

"What the fuck is your problem?"

She didn't answer. Instead, she swallowed some more water. Something was different about her behavior, and he couldn't put his finger on it. Why in the hell was she so damn antsy? He didn't want to keep arguing. Arguing with J.C., and now this bullshit. He left the kitchen without saying a word, and when he was about to exit her home she yelled out, "Tommy, I'm sorry!"

He looked back and made eye contact with her.

She set the water down on the coffee table then stepped to him, placing her arms around him. "Hey, I'm sorry, teddy bear." She smiled. "Yeah, you're my teddy bear." She closed her eyes, still holding on tight.

He sighed, still wondering what the fuck was up with her. She had never acted like this before.

She reached underneath his shirt and rubbed his chest. It aroused him a little, but, damn, he didn't know what was going to happen next. She was so damn erratic. "What's wrong, Summer?"

"Nothing is wrong," she said, but that was not his feeling.

She kissed him on the jaw and continued to rub his belly. He leaned toward her and grabbed her ass again, and she flinched again.

"Tommy, it's that time of the month."

"It's early." He had been dealing with her long enough to know just about when her period was due and how long it would last.

"Yeah, it's kind of early."

"Oh."

She shrugged. "Sorry."

"Is that why you been acting all funny and shit?"

"Possibly. I don't know." She released him. "I don't know, Tommy. I just have a lot on my mind."

"Talk to me."

"I don't know. I mean, I don't want to bother you with my problems."

"I'm here for you."

He met her eyes. They stared at each other for a long time before she said, "Tommy, you have problems of your own."

"That's for damn sure, but you listened to me. I have to be here for you. What's up?"

She walked away. "I just don't know about this whole writing thing. I mean, have you ever had a dream that you wanted something so bad but you just didn't know how to acquire it?"

"Baby, you can do anything."

"Tommy, I've failed at everything I've tried. I dropped out of college, all my sisters have degrees, and I'm the only one who doesn't. That's why I left Texas. I didn't want my parents to keep pointing out to me that I was a failure."

"Did they say that?"

"No, but they would say that I was the only one without a degree. Do you know how hurtful that was?"

"No. I mean, I can't really relate. I'm an only child."

She walked away, picked up the bottled water and took a drink. "Tommy, I may not be a writer."

"You can do it."

"I thought I could write a novel. It is hard as hell."

"What's hard about it?"

"I don't know. The words just aren't flowing."

"You can do it. I have confidence in you."

"Yeah, but when I write, and then I read other writer's stuff, my shit sounds terrible and corny."

"I think you need to write the whole book first, then fix it."

She looked surprise. "What the fuck" Tommy, are you a writer? That's the same advice I got from this instructor on the net."

"I don't write anything but letters to you."

She smiled. "Tommy, you're so smart."

"I wouldn't say all that, but I have a little bit of common sense."

She stood, walked toward him and wrapped her arms around him. "I'm sorry, teddy bear."

They kissed. Afterward, he said, "Could you kill that teddy bear shit?"

J-Black was in a gray Dodge Magnum with his Taurus 9mm. He had gotten it brand new, fresh out the box from a crack head. He had given the crack head an eight ball of coke for the gun, but he pistol whipped the man and kept the dope. He lit a cigarette and thought about the money he would receive for the job. This would be an easy job. Once he learned the whereabouts of his targets, he knew it would be a piece of cake. He puffed the cigarette then pulled the Dodge Magnum into a driveway with two other cars. He waited on his targets. They would be driving a gray Tahoe. He didn't know anybody who lived in the neighborhood. He'd gotten his information from a girl named Tangie who used to fuck Corey. J-Black had pretended to know him and casually mentioned his name in conversation because he knew Tangie's grandmother had lived in the neighborhood.

"Yeah, I used to like that buster," Tangie had said.

"Yeah. I did time with him."

"I didn't know he did time."

J-Black had to be quick on his feet. "Well, we were in the county jail together. Real easy going guy."

"The nigga's a robber."

"Yeah, but you know how it is" you can be one way in jail and then another way on the street."

She sucked her teeth. "I suppose."

"I need to know where he lives so I can repay him for the money he gave me to get out on bond."

"He lives on Merriman Avenue, at the end of the road in a yellow house with white trimming. You will see a Volvo station wagon in the driveway."

"Thanks, baby!"

The Volvo station wagon sat in the driveway along with a green Camry. J-Black wondered whose Camry was in the driveway. He decided to pull out of the driveway and drive to the top of the hill. Maybe he would see the SUV rolling around, or maybe he would see somebody who could tell him where the targets were.

A group of teens were rolling dice under a light pole. J-Black slowed down, scanning the ground for money. There were only a few fives and tens on the ground. Nothing worth robbing for. He wanted to jump out the car and ask about Mario and Puff, but he knew that as an outsider nobody would tell him anything. They didn't know him and this was their hood.

He rolled farther up the street. It started to rain lightly, and when he got to the top of the hill he saw a man walking. J-Black rolled the window down. "Hey. Need a ride?"

"No, I'm good."

"Do you know a guy named Mario?"

The man slowed down. "Why?"

J-Black pulled the gun and cocked it. "Stop or I'ma blow your fuckin' back out."

The man stopped. He held his hands in the air.

"Where the fuck is Mario?"

"I don't know."

"But you know him, right?" Still pointing the gun at the man, J-Black got out of the car.

"Y-yeah. That's my homie."

J-Black smiled. "Call him."

"I don't have no phone."

"What the fuck you mean you ain't got no phone? It's 2007, everybody got a fuckin' phone, nigga!"

"I don't."

J-Black dug into his pocket, pulled his cell phone out and was about to hand it to the man, then he heard "Big Thangs Poppin'" by TI playing. The music came from the pocket of the man's sweatpants. "Nice ringtone, player."

The man didn't say anything.

"Answer your phone," J-Black said.

"Hello," he said.

"Where you at?" A female's voice blurted out.

"Don't wait up. I'm gonna be late."

"Hang that goddamn phone up and get in the car. In fact, you drive the car."

J-Black got in on the passenger side, gun still pointed at the man.

"What is your name?"

"Ramel."

"Okay, Ramel. Want you to know everything is gonna be okay as long as you do what I say."

Ramel looked J-Black in his eyes but didn't say anything. His expression said that he was trying to see if J-Black was really a killer.

"Motherfucker, if you don't do what I say, I'ma shoot your bitch ass in the face." He smiled, then laughed out loud. "How would you like to take one between your eyes?"

"I don't want that."

"Your insurance policy paid up?"

"Why?"

"Just don't want your mama having no fish frys trying to get up enough money to bury you."

Ramel cranked up the car, then looked at J-Black again. "Where are we going?"

"Going to Mario's house."

"Come on, man. What's going on?"

J-Black slapped Ramel across his ear with the gun. "Nigga

don't question me. Just take me to his house." He dug into Ramel's pocket. Three twenty-dollar bills and a five. He put the money in his pocket then reached for Ramel's cell phone and scrolled through the numbers until he found Mario's. He dialed the number. When Mario was on the phone he handed the phone back to Ramel.

"What's good?" Mario said.

"Where you at?"

"I'm with Puff. We about to get something to eat."

J-Black snatched the phone out his hand, put it on speaker, then pointed, indicating that he wanted Ramel to pull over. When the car was off the road, he handed the phone back to him.

"Ramel, you there?"

"Yeah."

"You want to get something to eat with us?"

J-Black whispered, "Tell the nigga, yeah."

"Yeah."

"Where you at?"

The rain was pouring down hard now. There was no visibility through the windshield. J-Black turned on the wipers and the defogger.

"Tell me where you at?"

"In front of old man Sammy's house."

"Okay. I'll be there soon." Ramel hung up the phone.

J-Black said, "Okay, this is the plan: when your friends get here, you tell them to get in the car with us."

Ramel was shaking nervously, but he didn't say anything.

J-Black put the gun up to Ramel's temple. "Okay. Is that understood?"

"Yeah."

A few minutes later an SUV pulled up in front of the house. The men were looking around, as they didn't recognize the car. Ramel rolled down the window. "I'm right here. Get in the car with us."

"Okay. Let me take my truck to my mama's house," said Puff.

J-Black put the gun up against Ramel's ribs. "I swear to you

I will blow a hole in your side if you do one thing slick."

Puff went inside his mama's house.

Mario opened the door and got in the backseat of the car.

Mario and J-Black made eye contact.

J-Black introduced himself, "Just call me Black," he said. "What up?"

"Need to get something to eat man. Where are we going?" J-Black grinned.

"I don't know. I was thinking of this spot down in South Charlotte called Firebird's."

"Yeah," J-Black said. "What do they serve?"

"Steak."

The cold steel was up against Ramel's stomach.

Seconds away from death, he had a sister and a little brother and no kids. His mother and father had died in a car crash two years prior. How did this happen to him? He was a good person overall. He had dabbled in marijuana here and there to make ends meet, but he wasn't a drug dealer, nor had he been a shady character. He wondered how it came to this. How did he become so unlucky?

A few minutes went by and J-Black said, "Yo, what's up with ya man? What's he doing in there?"

Mario replied, "He said he was getting some money and probably his gun."

"Okay, I feel ya," J-Black said, thinking what that would mean for his mission. "So Charlotte is like that""you have to roll with heat out here?"

Mario said, "Hell yeah."

"You got a gun too?"

"No, I left mine at home."

"Do I need to go get one?" J-Black asked teasingly.

"So where you from?" Mario asked.

"Florida."

"What bring you up this way?"

"My job. I'm a carpenter by trade, and I know there's a lot going on here."

"You working?"

"Downtown, on some condos on Fifth Street."

Puff stepped out the house and ran to the car. When he got in the backseat, J-Black introduced himself.

"I'm Puff."

Ramel drove away to the end of the street, and when he was about to turn onto the next street, J-Black pulled out some weed""purple haze. "Y'all niggas smoke?"

Mario said, "Hell yeah," and pulled out some Vanilla Dutch Masters.

J-Black handed him the weed and said, "Let's blow one." He smiled. "But we need to go to a discreet location."

Puff said, "Pull down by the park, on the other side of Merriman Avenue."

Mario turned the back light on and began to roll the blunt, dumping the purple into the cigar.

"Ramel, why the fuck is you so quiet?" Puff asked.

J-Black nudged him with the gun, reminding him that if he was to do anything stupid his life would be over.

"Just trying to keep my eye on the road and watching out for the police."

Puff laughed. "J-Black, this is a scary-ass nigga."

J-Black already knew that. Puff wasn't telling him anything new.

When they reached the park, Mario had the blunt up to his lips, already smoking. He took two puffs then passed the blunt to J-Black, whose lips sucked up the blunt like a Hoover.

He passed the blunt to Puff then reached across Ramel, hit the child locks and drew the 9mm. Puff would get one toke before J-Black blasted him in the face. His brain exploded, spilling onto the window.

Mario tried to open the door but couldn't. The locks were on.

J-Black pointed the gun at Ramel. "Climb in the backseat with your friend."

"What's going on?" Mario said.

Ramel climbed in the backseat and fell on Puff's body.

J-Black needed time to think. He had two hostages and he knew that watching two men was more difficult than handling one. "First I need you to empty your goddamn pockets, Mario."

Mario pulled out a wallet and some coins from one pocket, and from another pocket he pulled out a chrome .380.

"I thought you didn't have a gun?"

"I didn't know you to be telling you my business, man."

J-Black smiled. "Now you know me. Give me the motherfuckin' gun."

Mario passed it to him.

J-Black wondered what to do next. He was a veteran in this line of work but it didn't get any easier. "Ramel, give me Puff's gun."

Mario was shaking and wondering what was going to happen next. "Hey, man, listen. I will give you whatever you want; just don't kill me. I have a family."

Ramel handed J-Black the loaded 9mm.

"This ain't about you," J-Black said.

"What do you want from us?" Mario asked.

"I want you to tell me where the fuck does Q live?"

"I don't know where Q lives."

"Big tall Quentin?" Ramel asked.

"Nigga, you know everybody." J-Black smiled. "A real fuckin' resource."

"No. I don't know where he lives."

"What the fuck did you mention his name for?" J-Black said.

Ramel turned to Puff. A few moments ago his friend was enjoying some greenery. Now he was gone. He didn't want to die.

"So, you going to tell me where the nigga lives?"

"I don't know where he lives," Mario said, his legs shaking. "If I knew I would tell you."

"The window is foggy and it's starting to smell like blood in here," Ramel said.

"You think you smell blood now just wait til' I blast your other friend if he don't tell me where Q lives."

"I don't know where he lives."

J-Black grimaced. "You think that motherfucker gives a damn about you?"

Ramel said, "I know where his man Country lives."

"Okay. Show me where he lives."

"It's in a gated community."

"I didn't ask you that. Take me there."

Ramel asked, "Who's going to drive?"

J-Black hadn't thought about that. He knew that one of them had to drive. He needed to be in the backseat. He got out of the car, still aiming his weapon and careful not to take his eyes off of either one of the men as he walked around the front of the car to the passenger side. "Okay, I want you to drive, playboy," J-Black, said cutting his eyes at Mario.

He unlatched the child locks and Mario got out of the car. "Hurry up, motherfucker," J-Black yelled. He knew Mario could run. But he didn't. He got behind the wheel of the vehicle like a good little boy scout.

J-Black walked around the front of the car to the back passenger door, opened it, and pushed the body over on the seat. Ramel scooted over as far as he could go.

When Mario cranked up the car, Ramel said, "The apartments are off Park Road."

"Okay," Mario said.

"No funny shit, nigga, or else."

The men rode in silence. J-Black thought about the money he would receive after all of this was over. He wondered where he would take the dead bodies, but he really wanted to know where Q was. He knew he could find him; then he would really get paid. He thought back to how he used to rob Tommy. If he didn't get Q, he'd find out where Tommy's stash was. Either way, it was going to be a profitable day for him.

When they got to the apartment complex, Ramel said, "Drive to the back. He lives all the way at the back; the last building on the left."

"How do you know his man stays here?" J-Black asked.

"My sister used to talk to him."

"You mean fuck him." J-Black laughed.

"Yeah."

"Okay, right there behind that black Suburban," Ramel said.

"Is that his truck?" J-Black asked.

"Yeah, and the silver Benz R350."

"Two trucks, huh?" J-Black made a mental note. These niggas were making money and he wanted in""not to be partners. He wanted his cut, just because he knew he had the heart to take it.

"Where is the apartment?" he asked.

"The bottom one on the left."

"Don't lie to me."

"I'm not lying," Ramel said.

"I don't like liars," J-Black said, looking down at the dead body. J-Black dug into a small tunnel that traveled through the center of Puff's head. Blood stained the chrome handgun. J-Black put the gun up to Ramel's nose. "Smell it."

"I've been smelling it for the past hour."

"Don't you love the way it smells?"

"No."

J-Black then attempted to put the gun to Ramel's lips. "You like the way it taste?" He laughed.

Mario glanced over his shoulder to look at the psycho in the backseat. What kind of man would play with a corpse? An insane man obviously. A man that nobody was safe around.

J-Black ordered Mario to drive.

"Where we going?"

"Westinghouse Boulevard."

24

Fifteen minutes later they pulled off the exit. J-Black ordered Mario to drive to the International Tire company. "Turn into that parking lot."

"What are we doing here?" Ramel asked.

Puff's upper body fell forward. J-Black grabbed his arm and sat him up. "We're going to get rid of our friend."

"What?"

The motherfucker was crazy, and nothing he said or did was logical. Ramel wished he hadn't been the lucky one walking in the rain that night. The day had started great for him""he had gotten a new job with a moving company and he had signed up for some classes at a community college"|never did he think it would end like this.

We're going to put him in the dumpster behind the building.

Mario slowed the car down. "Are you crazy, man?"

"Motherfucker, I'm calling the shots and I say drive to the back of the building!"

"Somebody is going to find the body."

"We're putting his ass in a trash compactor."

"What the hell?" Mario said, and turned the windshield wipers up higher. "I feel like I'm in a motherfuckin' movie."

"And I feel like I'm on a high," J-Black said. "A high and I don't ever want to come down."

Ramel drove to the back of the building. J-Black knew the area well. He had worked at International Tire for about three weeks. He had gotten the job through a temp service and he was fired for being tardy too many times.

When they were along the back of the building; they parked. J-Black got out of the car first and then ordered the two men to get the body.

"Come on. Couldn't we just dump him in the river?" Mario said, as he grabbed Puff's arm. "I mean, it's raining too hard out here for this shit."

"Nigga, I don't give a fuck about no rain. Do what I say before I blast you in the back of your head."

The two men tried their best not to fall as they carried the body. Their feet slid underneath them on the wet street.

When they reached the compactor, J-Black ordered Ramel to move the boxes that were on top. He threw them to the street. They would cover Puff.

Puff's body went in the compactor head first, and when he'd been covered by the boxes, J-Black turned the compactor on. The metal sheets went back and forth, pulverizing Puff's body.

When they were done, and as the three men were headed to the car, J-Black said, "I want to know where Q lives."

Mario said, "I don't know where he lives."

"Somebody knows."

"We don't know. Really," Mario said.

J-Black put the gun to the side of Mario's neck. "I wanna know where he lives, damn it," J-Black said, then slapped Mario in the face with the gun. "As a matter of fact, lay down." He then turned to Ramel. "You lay down, too."

"Please don't hurt us, man," Ramel said.

"Shut up and lay down."

Both men lay face down.

"Hands behind your head."

"Please. Please, don't hurt us," Ramel said, placing his

hands behind his head. He knew that if he obliged, there was at least a chance that he would be spared. At least that is what he thought.

Mario turned to look at J-Black's face. He then refused to turn over.

J-Black fired the gun at point blank range right between Mario's eyes.

When Ramel heard Mario scream, he prayed to God, but it was a wasted effort. J-Black fired two shots in the side of Ramel's temple. He checked the mens' pockets then left.

Minutes later, J-Black was in the driveway of Puff's mother's house. When she turned on the porch light and tried to identify him, he said, "Hey. I'm Puff's friend. I gotta flat tire. I need help."

When she opened the door, he cocked his gun. Her eyes grew.

He stepped in and closed the door. "Where is the goddamn money?"

"What money?"

"Your son's money."

She held her hands up.

"His room is in the back," she said, pointing.

"Who else is here?"

"Nobody."

He grabbed her and put the gun to her temple. His hand was around her waist. She was very soft and felt very good to him. She looked to be about fifty, but damn, she was in damn good shape.

"Walk me to his room."

Inside the room were piles of clothes""mostly urban stuff. And there were a couple of pairs of Nikes and Timberlands. The safe was in the corner. It was a small safe with the key still in it. Bingo""the stash.

J-Black opened the safe: A nine millimeter, a ski mask, and seven stacks of cash. He assumed they were thousand dollar stacks. "What the fuck? This ain't shit," he said angrily. "Where the fuck is the rest of the money?"

"What money?"

"Your son's fuckin' money, bitch."

"Hey. I don't know anything about no money. I didn't even know this was in here."

J-Black assessed the situation. Puff was a small time stick-up kid or else the ski mask would not have been there. He looked over at Puff's tiny twin bed, which was made up. He popped the rubber bands off the stacks and spread the money out on the bed.

"Have you ever fucked on a bed full of money?"

The woman was afraid. "Please don't do anything to hurt me."

He grabbed her ass. Damn, it was soft. This old bitch's ass was nicer than most girl's half her age.

"Please, Mister, don't hurt me."

He covered her mouth with his hand and shoved her to the bed. "Nobody is going to get hurt."

He had seen someone fuck before on a bed full of money; he couldn't remember who. But $6,000 wasn't any money at all; it was the fantasy that got him off. The money was power and his erection stiffened because the woman was helpless.

"Come on. I'm old enough to be your mama."

"But, bitch, you ain't my mama." He unbuttoned her blouse.

"Please, don't hurt me. What else do you want?"

He shoved her to the bed and unhooked her bra. "I'ma get me some of this pussy."

"God don't like ugly."

"I don't believe in God."

"Listen. No matter what you've done in the past, God will forgive you. He loves you."

Nobody loved him. No family, friends"|nobody. It had been a long time since anybody had even mentioned love to him.

"Do you want to be saved?"

He didn't bother to take his pants down. All of that God talk had turned him off. He gathered the money and banded it up. "I'm about to get the fuck out of here."

She smiled. "Thank you, sir. Remember, God loves you."

J-Black scurried to the front door. Puff's mother was behind him. Just as he was about to step out of the house, he said to her, "Oh yeah"¦I forgot to tell you. Your son won't be coming home tonight."

Dear Summer,

I know you haven't heard from me in a few days; been kind of busy lately, you know, trying to make that money, but I want to see you.

Have you seen that new Denzel Washington movie yet, "American Gangster?"

I heard it was pretty good. Hit me up if that's something you want to do. Let's make it a date. Let's go to Outback then the movie. Holla Back.

Q

25

The movie was over at midnight. Inside Q's BMW they talked about the film.

Q purposely held his right arm on the steering wheel, hoping she noticed his iced out bracelet that he had bought for thirty grand.

She stared at it, not because she liked it, but because she wanted him to feel important. "Thank you for the date, Q. I really liked the movie."

Q, still looking at the road ahead, cut his eyes at her and said, "I really like you."

She smiled. She knew he liked her, but she really wanted to know how much he liked her. She thought for sure that after they had sex he would disappear, but he was still coming around.

"I like you a lot," he said, putting his hand on her thigh.

"Nice bracelet, Q."

"Oh, this old thing? Yeah, I had it for a while."

"Yeah? It's very nice."

"Are you into jewelry?"

"I really don't know how to answer that one, Q. I mean, I like it, but I don't own a whole lot. I have other priorities to take care of first."

He smiled. "You know"|tell me what you like. I'll get you a bracelet. Is that what you want?"

"That's okay."

"Oh, you don't have to pay me back," he said, his hand now rubbing her pussy. He unbuttoned the top button of her blouse.

She turned to him and pointed. "Q, keep your eyes on the road."

He pulled over and drove behind a Value City furniture store.

He unzipped his pants then leaned into her and began to kiss her. His cell phone rang.

The caller ID read Country. He would call him back. He unhooked her bra.

Country called again. Q knew it was important. He answered.

"Nigga, it's bad now."

"What you talking about?" Q knew that whenever Country called, it usually meant one of his lieutenants was in trouble.

"Puff and Mario dead."

"What the fuck you mean they dead?"

"Mario and Ramel were shot in the head execution style and Puff's blood was found near the trash compactor."

"What?"

"Yeah."

"So what's up? Do they know who done it?"

"Puff's mom said some guy broke into her house and held her at gunpoint. She thinks that he was the same man that killed Puff."

"Why did she say that?"

"Because after the man robbed her he told her that her son wouldn't be coming home tonight."

"Are you serious?"

"Yeah."

"Was Corey with them?"

"No. He's the one that told me about it. Says it's been on the news all day."

Q's mind raced. "What the fuck? Who the fuck done this to them?"

"I don't know. Maybe Tommy had something to do with this."

"Yeah. That's what I was thinking," Q said, wondering how Tommy knew who fired shots at him.

"Baby what's wrong?" Summer asked.

He turned to her and at the same time he zipped his pants. "My friends" two of my friends are dead."

She grabbed his hand and held it. "I'm sorry, Q."

"It's okay," Q said as he looked into her eyes. But it was not okay. He had to find the men who killed his friends.

"We gotta get whoever done this," Country said.

"Yeah I know," Q said.

"Can I see you?"

"Maybe later. I'm kind of busy right now."

"It's about Ramel."

"What about Ramel? And why was he with them in the first place?"

"You know I used to fuck with his sister, and she is taking it hard."

"What you saying?"

"We have to find out who done this."

"I already know this."

"Can we talk now? I have some information."

"Okay. I'll meet you in twenty minutes at the Waffle House on Billy Graham."

Q terminated the call and then looked at Summer. "I have to take you home."

"Yeah. I heard. But when you finish your meeting I'd like to see you."

He leaned forward and kissed her. She held him. She didn't want to let him go.

The Waffle House on Billy Graham Parkway was almost empty. A trucker and two hookers were the only customers. Country and Q sat in the back of the restaurant.

"So you think Tommy had something to do with it?" Q asked.

"Hell yeah. I mean, two of the niggas that fired shots at him are dead."

Q took a deep breath. He really didn't think Tommy had the balls to have something like this done, but it really was too big of a coincidence. "But what did you need to talk about?"

"I think I know who actually did the killing."

"Who?"

"This nigga named J-Black, from North Charlotte."

"I've heard that name before," Q said, trying to figure out where he'd heard it.

"Yeah. He's a stick-up kid."

"Yeah. That nigga robbed me before."

"Oh yeah? You never told me that."

"Because he only got $97 from me."

"I don't understand."

"Yeah, he robbed the gambling house and he may have gotten about $15,000, but I only had $97. I had lost about five grand that night already. Ramel's sister had called and said that some girl said that J-Black bragged about doing it."

"Really?"

"Yeah. Can you believe this nigga?"

"Yeah, this man is a real killa. We have to figure out how to deal with him. I know" I think we can get the girl to help us."

Q placed his hand underneath his chin. "Who is the chick, and are you sure that she will help us?" he asked.

"Her name is Tangie."

"Where does she live?"

"I think she lives in Hidden Valley."

"A hood chick?"

"Yeah, but she seems to be cool."

"What you mean?"

"I talked to her on the phone and she seems like she is really upset about what happened," Country said.

A thin white waitress appeared, poured them both some water, then left.

Q took a quick sip then asked, "What the hell is she upset about?"

"She said that the nigga had been asking her questions about Mario and she said that she was the one that told him where he lived."

"So she was in on it?"

With his straw, Country stirred the ice in his cup. "No she wasn't. Says she didn't know what he was going to do."

Q looked Country directly in his eyes. "So do you believe the bitch?"

"Yeah."

"So my question is, What do we need to do?"

"I say we ask her to help us catch up with Mr. J-Black. Money talks and bullshit walks."

"What you talking about?"

"Give the bitch a few dollars. Pay her bills or something. I guarantee we can get our man," Country said.

The waitress dropped off two plates of pecan waffles then left.

Putting the syrup on his waffles, Q said, "I'm gonna get that nigga Tommy if it's the last thing that I do."

"Yeah. We gotta deal with him now."

Summer opened the door wearing nothing but a T-shirt with no panties. When she turned to walk away, Q grabbed her ass. When he took his hand off her ass, she said, "Damn. What did you stop for?"

"You horny, huh?"

She turned to face him. "Quit asking stupid questions."

He leaned into her and kissed her. Then he gripped her ass again.

"Damn, I like the way you hold this ass."

"That's my ass."

She laughed. "Is that so?"

"Yeah."

"Well handle this ass then." She lifted her shirt.

Her pussy was dripping wet. He grabbed her hand and lead her to the sofa. He kicked his shoes off; his pants and his shirt came off at the same time.

She dropped to her knees, pulling his member from his boxers.

Inside he smiled and thought about how good the sex would be. She wrapped her lips around his dick quickly.

"Yeah, baby I like that."

She looked up at him, and with the palm of her hand she gripped his balls gently. Pulling her lips away from his dick she teased him with her tongue.

"Put your lips back on it, baby."

She looked up into his eyes. Giggling, she said, "Say please."

"Please baby! Please!"

She took him in her mouth once more. Grabbing his dick she pulled it in and out of her mouth.

She placed his hand on her breasts, then she began to finger herself. She moaned and his dick stiffened.

The sound of his dick going in and out of her mouth sounded like a plunger unstopping a sink. She was trying to suck every inch of life out of his dick.

"I want you to suck my balls."

"Yeah baby," she said, and then licked his balls.

He concentrated real hard; his mind on the beautiful woman below giving him spectacular oral sex, but he couldn't seem to cum.

"Cum, baby! I need you to cum all over me."

As hard as he tried, he couldn't do it. He needed to be inside her. He pulled his penis out of her mouth. She stood up and he grabbed her legs, placing his tool in the middle. She screamed hard.

"Yeah, baby. Fuck the shit outta me!"

His hands slid from her legs to her ass. "This is my pussy."

"Yeah this is your pussy, Daddy."

"You like this dick don't you? Yeah."

"Turn me over and pull my hair."

He put her down and turned her around. She bent over while

standing, placing both hands on the sofa. He kept pounding away. Finally he slowed down.

She looked back. "What's wrong?"

"I'm about to cum."

"Cum inside me."

He didn't want to cum inside her, but he didn't want to take his dick out of that wet pussy either.

"Pull my hair, Daddy."

He stroked her hair then yanked it, wrapping it around his hand.

"Yeah."

"This is my pussy."

"Yeah, Daddy. I like when you talk dirty to me."

He slapped her ass, and when her cheeks jiggled it made his erection that much harder.

Reaching between his legs she grabbed his balls and he exploded inside her.

26

Scooter was doing about 72 miles-per-hour in a 65 when he got pulled. The cop, a young white guy, clean shaven and about 22-years-old, was looking at Scooter's license. "I'm going to need you to step out of the car."

Scooter knew what that meant from years of experience. He knew they were going to search his car. He was dirty, of course, but it was nothing he couldn't handle; only 25 pairs of counterfeit Nikes and some handbags. "I don't understand, Officer. What did I do?" Scooter was trying his best to be polite.

"Just step out the car, Mr. McKintosh."

"I don't understand?"

Seconds later the K-9 unit came, and a couple of plain-clothes officers.

"I know y'all motherfuckers don't think I'm no drug dealer," Scooter said.

A big black cop with a bald head ordered Scooter to step away from the car.

Minutes later, they had his backseat on the street. The young cop handcuffed Scooter, throwing him to the ground, scuffing his white T-shirt and crisp Air Force Ones.

"This is some bullshit!" Scooter yelled.

"Mr. McKintosh, I smelled marijuana in your car," the young cop said. "We're going to do a quick search. If nothing turns up, you can go on about your business."

"How the fuck you gonna smell marijuana and I don't even smoke?"

"We will see."

"You wasting your fuckin' time."

"Mr. McKintosh, could you just relax until we complete the search?"

Scooter frowned. "You can't tell me when to relax."

"One more word out you, we're going to take you downtown for disorderly conduct."

"I don't give a fuck," Scooter said.

The big cop with the bald head then stood Scooter and placed his hand underneath his chin, cutting off his blood circulation. He slammed him to the highway pavement as a car whisked by Scooter's head in excess of 65 miles-per-hour.

The K-9 officer was a red-headed man wearing a blue Charlotte Mecklenburg police coverall suit. His name tag read, Manning. He held tightly to the German Shepard as the dog explored the vehicle. The third row""25 boxes of Nikes and some knock off handbags. The rookie cop pushed that to the side. They would explore that later.

After searching the back and the front seat, the dog turned up no drugs.

"Mr. McKintosh, you were right. There are no drugs here," the rookie cop said.

"Why the fuck would I lie?" Scooter said.

"But what we did find was these counterfeit Nikes and some Western Union receipts to China."

"So what? I ordered some things off the Internet. Big fuckin' deal."

The bald guy stood Scooter up again.

"Yeah, counterfeit. This stuff is illegal," the rookie cop said.

Scooter looked the man in the eye. "So you gonna take me down for this bullshit?"

"It's illegal, Mr. McKintosh," the black cop repeated. He then walked Scooter to the squad car.

Scooter couldn't believe that these cops were this fanatical over some damn Nikes. He thought about the Western Union receipt. He had sent thousands of dollars to China for counterfeit goods during the past three years. He knew that if they checked thoroughly, they would find it was not just an Internet buy, but a real illegal business that he had organized. He vowed he would never sell drugs again after he was released from the feds, and he had made thousands of dollars in the counterfeit goods game. He had sold knock-off cell phones, golf clubs, guitars"¦never in his wildest dreams did he think he'd be going down for this.

At the police station Scooter was in a familiar place"¦the interrogation room. He had been there many times before from the age of fourteen. He sat across from two detectives, a black and a white. He knew the routine so well. They would play against each other to get the results they needed. The white cop wore a plain white shirt with jeans, and had identified himself as Myles. The black cop wore jeans as well. He was a light skinned man; well built. He didn't identify himself, nor did he smile. Myles started the conversation. "So you're in the shoe business?"

Scooter looked the man in his eyes. "Yeah, I sell shoes sometimes; a few pair here and there."

"The Western Union receipts were totaling about $30,000 this month."

"What's your point?" Scooter said.

The black cop still didn't say anything. He placed a yellow legal pad on the desk. Then he placed his pen there. Scooter noticed that it read Drug Enforcement Agency. Scooter made up his mind, right there on the spot, that he wasn't saying shit.

Myles asked, "Do you know selling counterfeit goods is illegal?"

"Yeah," Scooter said, not a hint of nervousness in his voice.

He'd been in the interrogation room for far worse crimes then this. They weren't going to break him.

"Yeah, it's a federal offense."

Scooter looked confused. "Yeah, but it's not a serious charge."

"Anything federal is serious."

"Yeah, but it couldn't carry much time""maybe none at all," Scooter said confidently. The first time he was locked down he had been caught with two kilos of coke. He would gladly march into federal court for a few pair of counterfeit Nikes.

The black cop finally spoke. "So, you've researched the guidelines?"

"No"!"

"Okay. Well, let me tell you, if this were your first offense, you would be right. But guess what, it's your third and we can consider you a career criminal."

"Who are you?"

"I am with the DEA."

"What the hell are you doing here anyway? I don't sell drugs."

The man laughed, dug into his briefcase and pulled out a manila envelope then set it on top of the notebook.

Scooter said, "I don't want to see no pictures. I don't know nobody."

"You want to do thirty years for some Nikes?"

"I'm not telling you shit."

"Your problems are more serious than some stolen Nikes," Myles said, smiling.

"What the hell are you talking about?"

Myles pulled out a pack of cigarettes from his drawer""Pall Malls. He lit one then offered it to Scooter who turned it down.

"What the hell are you talking about?" Scooter asked again.

"That nice Escalade of yours has been reported stolen."

"What the fuck are you talking about?" Scooter said.

"Who sold you the car?"

"Hey. I don't want to talk," Scooter said, knowing the car was stolen.

"Tommy sold you the car, huh Scooter?" said the black cop.

"What the fuck are you talking about?"

"I watched him sell you the car."

"Watched who sell me what?"

"Tommy Dupree sell you the Escalade."

"Who the fuck are you?"

"I'm Agent Mark Pratt of the DEA."

Scooter asked for a cigarette. Myles gave him one and lit it.

"So you want to help us, Scooter?"

He didn't say anything. He just breathed heavily and blew two large smoke rings out. He wondered if Tommy had given him up. Had he set the other guy up? Scooter had talked to Tommy about knocking Q off. He wondered how much of this the feds knew. Scooter reached for the ashtray. Pratt picked up his pen. "So, you know how it works; the first one comes forward with the information gets the best deal."

"I don't know what you're talking about. If you knew that the car was stolen why didn't you bust us then?"

"I didn't know what was going on. I actually thought it was a drug deal."

"So what do you want to know?" Scooter said.

"I want you to help me get Tommy."

"Get him for what?"

"Anything. I want to know what he's up to" is he selling drugs or what?"

Scooter stubbed the cigarette out. "I don't know anything."

Scooter's bail was set at $20,000. He bailed out. He had sixteen voice messages""fourteen of them were from J-Black, who wanted the money for the jobs he had completed. Scooter listened to the last message. "Yo Scooter, this is J, man. Y'all niggas are playing with my motherfuckin' money. I'm telling you, man, if you don't answer your phone, I'ma pay your mama's house a visit and when I leave it ain't gonna be good." Scooter called Tommy.

"Yo. What up, Scooter?"

"Long night."

"What happened?"

"I went to jail, nigga."

"For what?"

"I need to talk to you in person, man."

Seconds passed by. "Is it serious?"

"Yeah it really is."

Tommy sighed. "Okay. We can get together later tonight, maybe like nine."

"Cool. Also, that nigga J-Black been calling the shit out of me. I mean, I think he might have completed the job. He's making threats and all kinds of shit about his money."

"Okay, bring him with you when we meet."

"Okay, I will."

"Summer, this is bullshit and you know it," Tonya said, wheeling her BMW in and out of traffic. They were headed to the mall.

"What's bullshit?"

"This shit talking about you not liking Q."

Summer didn't say anything. She just continued to flip through an Essence magazine with Nia Long on the cover.

"Shit sounds like it's getting serious to me."

Summer looked up from the magazine. "I mean, he's just a booty call."

"But you like this booty call."

"You know what I like? I like his confidence."

"Yeah, and I know it don't hurt that he's a bad boy, too."

"Well, you know I like a little thug in them."

"What's up with Tommy?"

"The last time I talked to him he was pretty upset that his pops had stolen some money from him."

"Wait a minute. I thought his pops was rich" thought he had inherited some money or something."

"No, he was paid some money because he was falsely imprisoned."

"What happened to the money?"

"Tommy said he's on drugs."

"It's a damn shame to see black people come into money then don't know how to act when they get it."

"Yeah, I know what you mean."

Tonya turned into the mall parking lot and put the car in park. When both women were out of the car, Tonya asked, "So, is it over for you and Tommy?"

"Over? I don't know what you're talking about."

They reached the door of the Nordstrom's department store. Tonya stepped inside first. When Summer was inside, she said, "We were never together."

"Yeah, but he was kind of like ya man."

"I don't understand."

"He was the closest thing you had to a man, that's what I mean. He was kind of like ya man."

"I guess so," Summer said. She walked to the women's department and picked up a pair of black skinny jeans. She liked them, and wondered if Q would too.

"So, you know Tommy likes you."

Ignoring Tonya's last sentence Summer said, "Do you think these jeans will make my butt look big?"

"Get a size smaller," Tonya said.

Summer put the jeans on the rack and grabbed a size 6. She was really a size 8.

She always wanted to make sure her ass looked spectacular, even if it meant being a little uncomfortable.

"Summer, what are you going to do about that man's feelings?"

"That man has a live-in girlfriend."

"I know he does, but he still considers you his girl."

"I don't belong to nobody but Bobby Lee and Veronica, and they live in Missouri City, Texas."

"You know what I mean."

Summer flagged a salesperson and asked to be let into the dressing room. She wasn't in the mood to talk about Tommy. She stepped into the dressing room and stepped out with the jeans shellacked to her ass. "What you think?"

"I like them," Tonya said.

"Yeah. I need to pick out a blouse and a nice pair of heels to wear with these."

"So, which one of your men are you trying to dress up for,

Tommy or Q?"

"Why you keep talking about Tommy?"

"Because you know that man love you, Summer. And it seems like it's started to get serious with this Q guy."

Summer knew Tonya was right, and she knew that eventually she would have to tell Tommy about Q. She remembered the last time he visited and how she had to warn him not to show up at her apartment. He had acted a little suspicious. "So what do you think I should tell him?"

"Summer, do you think this Q guy is better for you?"

"What do you mean?"

"Do you think that he'd do the things that Tommy has done for you? Do you think he'd be the kind of friend Tommy is?"

"I don't know."

"But you like him don't you?"

"Yeah," Summer said, walking over to a rack of blouses. She wondered could she really depend on him. Tommy had proven himself time and time again.

27

When Summer got home, she pulled her Blackberry from her purse because it was vibrating. The caller ID said Tommy. At the last moment, Summer said, "Hey, baby!"

"Who the hell is this?" a female voice asked.

She knew that it was Tommy's live-in, Angie. She wanted to hang up in the woman's ear, but she didn't.

"Who the hell is this?" the voice repeated.

"My name is Summer," she said as she laid across her bed. She could hear pain in the woman's voice.

"What the hell are you doing texting Tommy?"

Summer contemplated. She hadn't text Tommy in a while. Tommy must have had old messages on his phone. "I don't know what you're talking about."

"I'm sure you don't. Just to let you know, Tommy is mine and he ain't going no where."

Who did this bitch think she was? She certainly didn't intimidate Summer. She wanted to laugh in the woman's face but she kept her cool. "Tommy's your man"¦really?"

"Yes, my fiancé."

Though Summer was now sleeping with Q, she became furious, not because what Angie said, but because it was obvious Tommy had been promising that he was going to marry this woman.

"Yeah. We're getting married next year."

"Congratulations."

"Who are you?"

"Just call me the side bitch," Summer giggled.

"Leave him the fuck alone."

"Who the fuck are you to tell me to leave anybody alone?"

"I'm his future wife."

"Hmph. That ain't what he told me."

"What did he tell you?"

"He ain't tell me nothing about you, that's for damn sure."

"Really?"

"Yeah, really."

"Tommy doesn't love you, he loves me and I will prove it to you."

"How?"

"Hey, just stay on the phone and be quiet," Summer said. She felt bad for even entertaining this broad, but she had to let this chick know she was not number one, even though she was no longer sure she wanted to be with Tommy. She dialed Tommy on the three-way.

Tommy answered on the first ring. "I was just thinking about you."

"Really?"

"Yeah."

"What were you thinking?" Summer said. She felt like she was betraying him but she just couldn't get Angie's words out of her head.

"I was thinking about us."

"Us?"

"Yeah. I mean, I haven't spoke with you in a while and I was wondering how you are doing?"

"What are you talking about? You were over my house last week"¦ remember? You were telling me about your father and his drug problem."

Tommy sighed. "Yeah."

"So what's going on with him? Is he doing okay?"

"Yeah. I guess. Haven't seen him in a while."

"Why not, Tommy? He's your father."

"I know, but I have a lot of other shit on my mind."

"Like what, Tommy? You know you can tell me anything."

"I know. That's why I like you."

"Tommy, I'm sorry about what happened the other night."

"Yeah. What was that all about? You ain't never trip before when I came over to see you."

"I know. It's hard to explain. I mean, I was kind of emotional, you know? My period was about to come on."

"Whatever, man. You just snapped on me for no reason."

"You think I really snapped on you?"

"Hell yeah."

"Tommy, let's not argue. I want to talk seriously for a minute."

"What you want to talk about?"

"I think you were out of line when you came over the other night."

"What? I thought you were sorry about what happened the other night."

"Tommy, cut the bullshit. I'm a woman. I'm an emotional being."

"This shit don't make no sense to me. I mean, you blame your actions on your period and now you are bringing the same bullshit up."

"I know you don't understand. You wouldn't."

"So what's this all about?"

"I want to date other people."

"What the fuck. Where did that come from?"

"I do, Tommy. I mean, you got your woman, what's her face"¦" Summer said. She knew Angie's name, had heard all about her, but she couldn't let Angie know she had actually given her a second thought.

"Who are you seeing?"

"What difference does it make?"

"Yo, that's really fucked up."

"Tommy, where could me and you possibly go in this relationship? I mean, you aren't going to leave your woman."

Summer heard Angie breathing on the phone. Tommy probably heard it too but he would just assume it was Summer.

Tommy said, "You don't know what I'm going to do."

"You're not going to leave her. If you were going to leave her you would've left her by now."

"It's not that simple, Summer."

"I know." Summer paused and thought. She really wanted to make Angie mad, but how?

"Me and Angie got a lot of history together, Summer."

"Yeah, I know. And me and you are moving in two different directions."

"How so?"

"Tommy, I want to get married one day and I just don't think you're the right one. I mean, I don't think that you want to marry me."

"That's not true."

"Tommy, do you love me?" Summer said, wondering if Angie had dropped the phone a long time ago. She'd hoped that the bitch was reduced to tears. She could picture tears rolling down those sweet little cheeks.

"Tommy, are you there?"

"Yeah."

"I asked you a question."

"I know you did."

"And what is your answer."

"Summer, you know I love you."

"Tommy, what the fuck did you just say!?" Angie interjected.

"Who is this?" Tommy asked, but he already knew. It sounded like Angie, but how? Why? How much had she heard? Tommy terminated the call.

Tommy's phone rang several times but he didn't answer. He needed time to think. He couldn't believe this was happening to him. What had gotten into Summer? How did she and Angie meet? Had they met? Would Angie have his baby now that she had heard him say that he loved another woman? A woman who obviously didn't love him or else she wouldn't have set him up like that. Were Summer and Angie together? Were they friends now? Who initiated the conversation? Which one of them was out to get him? Had they both gotten fed up with his B.S.? The phone rang. It was Summer. He sent her straight to voice mail. It rang again. This time it was Angie. He didn't answer it either. Summer sent him a text message"¦Tommy call me I need to talk I'm alone.

He responded. What the fuck do we need to talk about? He didn't believe she was alone. Those bitches had to be in this together.

28

It was 2:00 a.m. J-Black drove the Dodge Magnum down I-77, headed to the Waffle House. He would get some breakfast before turning in. It had been a long night with little reward""two home invasions that netted him $3,000. "Broke-ass drug dealers"¦" he mumbled to himself.

His phone rang. It was Tangie. He answered.

"Hey, baby. I want to see you. Can we get together?" she said.

"I'm not meeting with you unless I'm getting some pussy."

"Don't worry, baby. I'm going to take care of you," Tangie said.

"But yesterday you said you were on your period."

"It stopped today, and I'm just so goddamn horny."

"Where you at?" he asked. Suddenly Waffle House wasn't that important. He would get the bitch to cook him something right after she gave him head.

"The Pointe Apartments on Tyvola."

"Yeah? What the fuck you doing over there?"

"My auntie's house."

"Your auntie's house? What the fuck do you mean, your auntie's house? I know your aunties; both of them, and don't neither one of them live on no Tyvola."

"Not my mama's sisters, silly, my daddy's sister. My aunt Jene."

"She got food? Because I'm hungrier than a motherfucker."

"She cooked some baked chicken today. I'll heat it up for you."

"Okay. I'll be there in twenty minutes."

"Enter from the back gate, the Nation's Ford Road entrance."

J-Black pulled up to the gate. A security box was at the gate, which required a code for entrance; one that he didn't know. He called Tangie. She didn't answer. He dialed again. Still no answer. Where in the hell is she? Why ain't she picking up the phone? Maybe the bitch is in the shower. Damn, that baked chicken sounded good. Some rice would be nice with that, and a glass of iced tea, he thought. Then he would fuck the shit out of Tangie. She wasn't much to look at, but damn, she could fuck. Had been fuckin' since she was fifteen, so she had told him.

He tried dialing her number again. No answer. When he put the Magnum in reverse, he looked in the mirror. That is when he saw the first man behind him. The second man he didn't see until he was next to the driver-side door.

Shots came through the back window first, shattering it.

J-Black tried to duck. He reached for the gun on his waist. That is when the second goon opened fire, shooting him twice in the side. J-Black slumped over.

The man shot two more times, once in his thigh and once in his lower leg.

The first goon was now on the passenger side. He fired two times, both shots hit J-Black""in his shoulder and in his back.

The goons then ran to a blue SUV that awaited them. The truck sped off. Nobody saw a thing.

J.C. offered his truck keys to Scottie in exchange for a quarter of an ounce of cocaine.

"I'm keeping it until Monday and then you pay me. Right?"

"Yeah."

"Make sure you have my money or else you ain't getting this nice-ass Range Rover back."

"I will have the money, no problem."

"Okay. Here you go. Pure Fiscale."

J.C. grinned, examining the bag. He couldn't wait to get home, but first he would trade some of his coke for some ecstasy. Then he would call Shantell.

Shantell picked up the phone. "Hello, Daddy."

"Hey baby, I got something for you."

"What you got?"

"I got some skittles," he said, using the street term for Ecstasy.

"What else you got for me?"

"What do you mean?" J.C. asked. He knew what she wanted. What she always wanted""money, and he didn't have any.

"You know what I want, Daddy."

"No, I don't," J.C. lied.

"Daddy, I need some help with my bills."

"Shantell, I don't have any money."

"Daddy, I only need $200."

"I don't have it."

"Aw, Daddy. Why are you treating me like this?"

"Come see me," he said. He didn't want to hear her whining.

"I don't want to see you."

"Why?"

"Because you ain't got no damn money."

"So, is this all this relationship been about?"

"You know it. I mean, what else can it be about, old man? I know you didn't think I loved you."

J.C. bit down on his lip. He didn't know what to say. He

knew that Shantell had only hung around him for money, but it just hurt so much to hear her say it.

"Goodbye, J.C."

"Take care, Shantell."

29

Tommy was staying at the Microtel Inn on Billy Graham when he received the call from Scooter. "J-Black got shot last night, and the doctors are saying that the nigga might not make it."

"What?" Tommy said more out of surprise than hurt or anger. For a brief moment he wished that J-Black would die. He had robbed him in the past, raped his ex-girlfriend and killed one of his friends. He was not somebody Tommy was very fond of.

"Yeah. He got shot last night entering the gate of some apartments. Some man discovered him slumped over in his car."

Tommy stood and began pacing. He wondered if Q had him shot. He didn't know what to do. He didn't want to go to the hospital to see J-Black. They weren't friends. He looked on the bright side, if J-Black died, there would be no chance of a murder-for-hire charge. Though he never thought it would come down to that anyway. Nobody knew J-Black had killed three niggas for him. At least he hoped they didn't.

"Damn. So, they have any idea who did it?"

"No, you know how it is. This guy had plenty of enemies. It could have been anybody."

"So they saying that he might not make it?"

"Yeah, man. This shit's crazy, man. Shit is going from bad to worse."

"You can say that again," Tommy said, thinking about all his problems. J-Black was the least of his worries.

"I think I might go to the hospital to see him," Scooter said.

"Keep me updated."

Friday night, and the AMC movie theater was full of teenaged kids. Q met one of the goons in the parking lot. The man was about five foot nine with a full beard. He was from Philly. That was the only thing Q knew about him. He'd been sent down by his cousin Eli from Norristown, Pennsylvania. The goon said, "The job is done."

"Good."

"Yeah, got that nigga good."

Q handed him a Nike shoebox stuffed with cash.

The goon looked. "I ain't got to count it, do I?"

"No. The money is good. You can trust me."

The man pulled his beard, contemplating. "No, I can trust Eli. I don't know you, nigga."

"How many times did you shoot him?"

"I don't know, maybe six or seven."

"Are you sure he's dead?"

"If that nigga lived, he's Superman."

Q shook hands with the goon.

Before the bearded man left, he said, "If you need me for anything else, just let Eli know. This is what I do." With the box still under his arm, he continued, "I'm also in the collection business."

"The collection business? What are you talking about, the collection business?"

"Yeah. You need me to collect some money, just let me know. If I don't come back with the money, you ain't got to pay me shit."

Q smiled, thinking there were a few outstanding debts out there. But it really wasn't worth hurting somebody over.

"I'll keep that in mind."

Q walked back to the SUV. Country fired it up. "Nigga said J-Black is dead."

"Cool."

"Yeah. Said they hit him up seven times."

"Dayum," Country said, pulling out of the parking lot. "We gotta take care of that Tangie, and then we're done. Right?"

"We have to take care of one more thing."

"What's that?"

"We have to send Tommy's fat ass a message," Q said.

Country pulled out of the parking lot and turned onto South Boulevard.

"What did you have in mind?"

"I'ma shoot his house up," Q said, pulling out a chrome nine.

"Why didn't you get those Philly niggas to do that?" Country asked.

"Because we can do that shit ourselves."

"Okay, when you wanna handle that?"

"I want to handle that shit right now."

"It's only eleven now."

"Well in another two hours."

"Do you know where he lives?"

"Yep, I got a bitch that work at the highway department to run his name."

"Damn nigga, you're a cold ruthless motherfucker."

"You already know this."

30

Tommy was at the Microtel sound asleep with CNN playing in the background when his phone rang. The caller ID read Angie. His gut told him something had happened. He answered the phone on the second ring. "What?"

"What my ass. Somebody just shot my house up."

Tommy sat up in the bed. "What you mean, somebody shot your house up?"

"Just what I said, Tommy. The police are here now asking me a bunch of questions and shit."

"I'm coming over."

"Hurry up, Tommy, hurry," Angie said with her voice full of emotion.

Tommy stood, still half asleep, and then he sat on the bed. He slipped into his pants and put his Jordans on thinking about the payback. He knew it had to be Q, and with J-Black in the hospital he would have to do it himself.

When he got there Angie was walking around in her robe, hair disheveled, showing the crime lab detective where the shots went. Tommy attempted to hug her.

She pushed him away. "Tommy please get the fuck off me."

The detective, a tall white man with glasses, asked Tommy, "Do you live here?"

"Yes."

"But you weren't here tonight."

"No."

"Okay, do you have any idea who might have done this?"

"No," Tommy lied. There was no doubt in his mind that Q had something to do with this.

"You have any enemies?"

"Not that I know of."

The man scribbled in the pad. A short Asian cop walked up with some casings. "Looks like one of the guns was a 40 caliber."

Tommy said, "One of the guns?"

"Yeah, there were at least 25 shots fired, and there are two different size holes in your wall."

"Damn."

"Yeah, looks like somebody is trying to send a message to you," the Asian cop said.

"Hey, it could have been the wrong house; I don't have any enemies."

The white cop shrugged. "Yeah, it could have been the wrong house, but highly unlikely. My experience tells me that it's somebody that you know."

Tommy looked the man in his face. Damn cops always think they are so goddamn smart. He walked away before the cop called out to him. "Sir, I need to ask a few more questions."

Tommy turned and faced the man.

The cop was still scribbling on his pad. "Where were you tonight?"

Tommy looked confused. "What does that have to do with anything?"

"Answer the question."

"I was at the Microtel on Billy Graham."

"Who were you with? Can anybody prove you were there?"

Angie stared at Tommy.

"I was alone."

"Why were you there in the first place? You live here."

Tommy looked at Angie. "Me and my girlfriend are not on good terms."

Angie said to the officer, "That's true."

"I don't know, maybe the front desk clerk," Tommy said, remembering that he'd lost his key and had to get a replacement around 11 p.m. "Yeah, the front desk clerk. I don't remember her name but she was a short little redhead."

"Sir, where do you work?"

"I don't."

The officer looked at the Range Rover that Tommy had just pulled up in.

"My pops sued the state and received a lot of money."

Angie said, "It's true."

"So, no job?"

"Well, I invest in real estate."

"I had a feeling you were going to say that."

"What is that supposed to mean?"

"Nothing," the man said, then handed Tommy his card. "If you hear of anybody talking in the street give me a call."

"Okay."

After taking more pictures and walking around the entire house twice, the officers interviewed the neighbors and then left.

Tommy walked inside the house behind Angie.

"Tommy, you know it's over now."

He saw the seriousness in her eyes. He attempted to put his arms around her. "Get the fuck away from me, Tommy."

"Hey, baby, I'm sorry. I am really sorry."

"Yes, I hate you." She burst into tears.

"I don't know who did this but I'm going to find out."

"Find out? Tommy, do you know I could have been killed?"

He was silent. What she was saying was right. He wanted to argue but what would be his point?

"Somebody wants you dead, and God obviously wants you alive, Tommy. You need to take heed and get your shit together."

He put his arms around her. "I know, baby, I'm going to do better. I'm through with this lifestyle."

She looked up at him. "And who the hell is this Summer girl?"

He took a deep breath but didn't respond.

"You love her, Tommy? Do you fuckin' love this bitch?"

"No."

"You're lying, Tommy. I heard you say that you loved her. Do you know how hard it was for me to listen to you say that you loved this girl?"

"I know, I don't know what I was thinking."

"Tommy, you said that shit out of sincerity. I heard the truthfulness in your voice."

"No I didn't. I love you, and I want you to have my baby." He attempted to feel her stomach, but she pushed his hand back.

"Tommy, I don't think there's going to be a baby."

"You're not pregnant?"

"I don't know."

"Still haven't taken the test?"

"No."

"What's taking you so long?" he asked, and then he began pacing.

"I don't want to find out, Tommy. I don't want to know if I'm pregnant. I told you I'm scared."

"Scared of what?"

"Of raising a child by myself."

He looked confused. "Raising a child by yourself? What the hell are you talking about?"

She held the palm of her hand up to his face. "Tommy, can you just go please? You have done enough."

"You want me to leave?"

"Hell yeah."

"Why? I want to stay."

"I don't think I'm going to stay here, thanks to you. I mean, some of your hooligan buddies have shot up my goddamn house. Do you know how embarrassing this shit is?"

He looked her directly in her teary eyes. "Hey, I'm really sorry this happened."

"I know you are. You're always sorry, but how in the hell can I live here now? My neighbors are going to be looking at me thinking somebody is after me and wondering what kind of shit I'm involved in."

He grabbed her hand and held it.

"It will never be the same, Tommy. You and I will never be the same."

He let go of her hand and held her face, forcing her to look at him. "I love you."

"Yeah"|maybe so, but you love that bitch Summer as well."

Tommy looked over the bridge again. If he jumped, he would want to die instantly. He didn't want to suffer, but he felt he deserved to suffer for what he'd done to Angie; what he'd done to his life. Hell, he was already suffering. Damn, he'd always considered himself a smart guy. People had told him that he wasn't living up to his potential, and he hadn't. He remembered the seventh grade""advanced biology. His teacher had told the class, "You're some of the brightest kids in the school district and you can be anything you want to be, and most of you will. Some will be scientists, doctors, attorneys, engineers. This is a great class I have here. Ten students in here have the highest GPA in the school."

Tommy wasn't one of the ten smartest kids in the school, but he was in the class with them and he'd passed the advanced biology class with a B, trigonometry with a B, and he'd had a 3.2 grade point average. But then, something went terribly wrong. Crack came and he saw his neighborhood turn into a haven for drug addicts. Rather than be an addict, Tommy decided he would capitalize off the demand for drugs. He'd started off selling crack to buy Jordan tennis shoes. When he'd gotten older, the sneakers were no longer important""cars were, and he needed to sell weight to buy cars. So he'd graduated from the corner hustler to a neighborhood supplier, and somewhere along the line, he'd lost his peace of mind and sanity.

He looked down at the rocks under the bridge. The tide was pretty low, meaning, he'd probably die pretty fast today. His seed was in Angie's stomach. He thought she was pregnant, but she hadn't found out. He thought about a little him; the thought brought a smile to his face. He couldn't kill himself""not just yet. He had another chance at life. One that he would live through his child.

Q and Country were sitting on the hood of his car in front of his mama's house serving packets when Danny the white boy came up with two Ipods. "Can I get a pack?"

Q turned to Country. "How much are these shits worth?"

"About $200."

"These are four gigabytes," Danny said.

"What the fuck does that mean?" Q laughed.

Danny looked as if he were trying to figure out a way to explain what gigabytes meant in a way that Q would understand, but not be offended. Finally he said, "It's worth maybe $250 before taxes."

"I'll give you three rocks for them both and that's all you getting from me."

"Come on Q, man. If you give me at least eight, you can have them."

"Five."

"Six."

Q turned to Country and said, "Give this fool six packs so he can get the hell out of here."

Country disappeared into a path behind Q's mama's house. When he returned, a black Range Rover had pulled up. Q pulled his gun when he saw Tommy get out.

"Nigga, what the fuck are you doing here?"

"I came to talk to you, Q."

"Talk to me? It's too late to talk," Q said, then cocked his gun.

Tommy threw his hands up in the air. "So what you gonna do, Q, shoot me in front of your mama's house?"

"How the fuck do you know this is my mama's house?"

"I know everything, Q."

"Nigga, you're a snitch. You're the reason my man is fucked up. I know it."

"That's one thing I'm not Q, is a snitch."

Q pointed the gun at Tommy.

"Shoot me, nigga."

Country grabbed Q and pulled him to the side. "What the fuck? Are you crazy, nigga? You can't shoot this man in front of your mama's house with a witness right here." Country pointed to Danny.

"Can we talk?" Tommy asked.

"What you want to talk about?" Q said.

Danny said, "Can I get my packs so I can be outta here?"

Country gave Danny the six rocks and he disappeared.

"You selling white kids packs?" Tommy asked.

"What the fuck do you care?" Q said.

"That motherfucker looks like he's barely 18-years-old."

"How the fuck you gonna tell me what to do, nigga? Just cause the feds got your punk ass don't mean they gonna get me."

"You think I'm the police?" Tommy said.

"All I know is my man is in jail right now because of your ass."

"And you just sold some packs to a white boy in front of me."

"Your point?"

"My point is, nigga, you don't believe that I'm the police."

Q stared Tommy in his eyes. "What the fuck are you here for?"

"I just want this shit to end."

"Why?"

"Your people shot in my girl's house last night and she ain't got shit to do with us."

"Three of my friends are dead," Q said.

"I ain't kill nobody," Tommy said.

"I know your fat ass ain't shoot nobody, and the punk ass shooter probably regretting that he killed my niggas."

Tommy became serious. "Q, can we let this shit end?"

Q stared at Tommy for a long time. "I'm going to count to four, and if you ain't outta here I'm blasting you, nigga."

"It's like that?"

"1"|2"|"

Tommy got into the Range Rover and drove away.

31

Dear Summer,

That was some foul shit you done to me the other day. I never thought it would get down to this. Why? What did I do to deserve this? So I guess you're happy now that you ruined me and Angie's relationship and it's obvious that you don't want me now. Deep down in my soul I know there is someone else in your life. Why don't you keep it real? Why won't you answer my calls?

Tommy

Sent via Sprint PCS Blackberry

Against the doctor's orders, J-Black checked out of the hospital. The doctor had said, "Go home and take it easy."

J-Black nodded, but he knew there would be no taking it easy. He had work to do. He had to repay the people who'd done this to him if it was the last thing he ever did in his life.

He sat in the wheelchair in front of the hospital when his stepsister Syreeta pulled her Honda Accord up to the door.

Barely able to stand, he hobbled to the car and closed the door. "Take me home," he said.

"But the doctor said that you need someone around you."

"I don't give a fuck what the doctor said. I want to go home."

Syreeta was a few years older than him. She was the only relative that he was close to. Her mother had married his father. Though they weren't biological brother and sister, they were very close. She was the only person in the world that he trusted.

She looked at him oddly. "Jason, what are you going to do at home by yourself?"

"I just want to be at home and sleep in my own bed, you know?"

She didn't respond. She just stared. She had known him long enough to know he was plotting some kind of revenge.

He smiled a little bit then he held his side.

"What's wrong, bro'?"

"Nothing."

"You're in pain?"

"I'm going to be okay. It just hurts a little bit where the staples are, you know."

"Yeah I can imagine."

"But I'm still here."

"Yeah, that's the main thing, Jason. You need to get yourself right with the Lord because he spared you for some reason."

"Those coward-ass niggas couldn't sleep. That's what that was all about."

"Give God the glory."

"Give those niggas some caps in they ass is what I'm going to do."

"I'm taking you to my house. I will not let you out of my sight because you're going to get yourself in some trouble."

"Take me home," J-Black demanded.

Syreeta ignored him. Fifteen minutes later she was pulling up in front of her house.

Tommy entered his father's house. J.C. was sitting on the sofa watching CNN. He looked up at Tommy but didn't say anything. Tommy sat on the sofa across from him. After a few minutes of silence, he said, "Hey, I want to apologize for how I treated you the other day."

J.C. smiled. "It's nothing, son. You had a right to be mad at me. I shouldn't have taken your shit."

"No," Tommy said. He grabbed the remote control that was on the table and turned the television down. "I didn't have to talk to you like that."

"I shouldn't have stolen your money, son. And I'm going to pay you back. I promise."

"You don't have to. Don't worry."

"I want to."

"Only thing I want you to do is get off the dope."

"I can't beat it, son."

"What you mean?"

"It's got a stronghold on me."

"You can get off it, Pops. It's just a mind thing. Just like everything else."

"And that's why I can't get off it, son. That's all I think about day and night; where my next rock is coming from."

Tommy looked at his father and tried to understand how he ended up like this. What made him try it? He was weak. Never had he seen him like this.

"I want to help you."

J.C. smiled again then stood and walked over to embrace his son.

"But first, you're going to have to want to help yourself."

"I do."

"You can beat it, Pops."

"I don't know, son."

"I'm going to help you. I'm going to help you because I want you to live. I want you to live to see your grandchildren."

"What you talking about?"

"Angie may be pregnant."

"I'm happy for you."

"Don't be happy. We don't know yet. Notice I said she might be pregnant."

"When will you find out?"

"I don't know. She's mad now."

"Son, what did you do to her?"

Tommy looked away from his father. He didn't know where to begin.

"You cheated on her?"

"Yes and no."

"I don't understand."

"That's part of the problem, but it's not what she's mad about."

"Well, you don't have to tell me if you don't want to."

"Pops, some niggas shot her house up looking for me."

"What?"

"Yeah."

J.C.'s eyes became serious, and he now had a concerned look on his face. "Why are they looking for you?"

"Long story short, they said they thought I snitched on their partner."

"That's ridiculous."

"And they know it's ridiculous. I just seen the niggas a few hours ago, and they were serving crack right in my face. How you going to sell dope around a snitch?"

J.C. disappeared to his room and came back with a .45. "It's yours if you need it."

"I don't."

J.C. embraced Tommy. "Son, I don't want nothing to happen to you. We are all we got."

"Nothing's going to happen to me."

Matt heard a loud knock on his door. He rolled out of the bed and saw the police in his driveway. He called Jay. "Hey, the cops are outside my house."

"Pretend you're sleep. They'll leave a notice on the door."

"That's the dumbest advice I've ever heard."

"Well open the door."

"What do you think they want?"

"How the hell do I know?"

Matt peeked out the window. They were knocking on

everybody's door in the cul-de-sac. Matt felt good. Maybe they were looking for a kid or something. He opened the door. The tall redhead cop introduced himself as Officer Tenent, and his partner, the black guy, was named Rainer.

"What can I help you with?"

"Looking for a stolen Yukon," Rainey said, his face was very serious.

Tenent looked Matt directly in his eyes. "You wouldn't happen to know where the car is?"

"Why you asking me?"

"We're asking everybody over here. We're getting a signal that the car is in the area."

"A signal?" Matt said.

"Yeah from the tracking device."

"Mind if we look in the garage?" Tenent asked.

Matt didn't answer. He didn't know how to answer. He didn't want to lie to the cops, but he knew that they knew the car was in the area. He knew the neighbors would probably volunteer to let the cops look in their garage; they had nothing to hide.

"Follow me," Matt said. They walked through the living room. When he opened the door leading to the garage, he'd wished the car would disappear but it didn't.

The two officers looked at each other. Neither said a word. Finally, Tenent said, "Whose vehicle is this?"

Matt took a deep breath. "This is what you're looking for?"

"Obviously," Rainer said.

"So you want to tell us about it?" Tenent asked.

"I-I bought it from Atlanta."

"Really?" Rainer asked. His voice was hard to discern. Matt couldn't tell if he believed what he said or not.

"Yeah, I bought the truck from somebody I met on the Internet."

"What's his name?"

"Am I under arrest?"

"No."

"I want to talk to my lawyer."

Rainer picked up his radio. "Lt. Grayson. I need you to call in permission for a search warrant of a residence."

"You can't do that."

"Watch me," Rainer said, then held the radio to his mouth again. "The address is 12087 Woodview Lane."

Matt knew that if they got the search warrant they would find titles for a few stolen cars that were in his name, and he had at least twenty sets of keys.

Rainer said, "It will take us about thirty minutes to get the verbal search warrant." He smiled confidently.

Matt knew that his scheme had come to an end. It was back to the feds for him. Wondering how this happened, he realized somebody had forgotten to disable the GPS. What the fuck was he going to do next? He wanted to say that it was a terrible misunderstanding, but how could he explain this? He stepped back inside and sat at the bar in the kitchen. He was going to jail. There was no getting around it.

32

Matt was surprised when the black man introduced himself as a DEA agent. Not because he was black, but because he was the DEA. Matt had never sold drugs in his life. The agent was a clean-cut boyish looking man, but Matt could tell he was older than him; maybe late thirties. "My name is agent Mark Pratt, Matt."

Matt dropped his face into his hands.

"I'm here to help you, Matt."

Matt looked up briefly then he thought about the marijuana plant he had been growing in the attic. That is what this is all about. It had to be. He would say that he didn't know a thing about the plant. It must have been in the attic when he'd moved into the place.

"What do you want with me?" Matt asked.

Pratt stared at Matt for awhile before saying anything. He was sizing him up and trying to figure out if Matt was a good person. Finally Pratt said, "I want you to go home."

Matt smiled. "I sure as hell want to go home."

Pratt looked at a folder. "You were in a few years ago for bank fraud."

"Are you asking me?"

"I'm telling you, the information is right in front of me."

"What the hell are you here for? Is it that measly fuckin' marijuana plant in my attic?"

"No."

"Then what is it? You're the DEA, I don't understand."

"Do you know Tommy Dupree?"

Matt took a deep breath, then he thought about the meeting he and Tommy had about Tommy's friend getting caught with the dope. Maybe somebody had forgotten to disable the GPS system in his friend's vehicle too. Maybe he was the reason Tommy's friend had gotten busted.

"I think you already know that I know him."

"So what's your affiliation?"

"We done time together you know we're just friends."

Pratt's face hardened. "Listen, Matt. Cut the bullshit. You're about to be indicted for running an auto theft ring."

"I still don't understand."

"Are you trading cars with Tommy for dope?"

"No."

Another man entered the room""a tall blondish guy about thirty. He shook Pratt's hand then flashed his badge. "I'm agent Connor of the F.B.I." Connor offered his hand to Matt, but he declined.

When Connor sat down, Matt said, "We didn't trade drugs for cars."

Connor opened a briefcase and presented Matt with pictures of three cars""a BMW and two Benzes. "Recognize any of these?"

"Why would I recognize them?"

Connor's face became stern. "Because you stole them, that's why."

"Hey, I want my lawyer."

"Matt, your lawyer's not going to be able to help you now."

"What do you mean?"

Pratt's Nextel chirped. He held the phone to his mouth. "Let me call you back. I'm in the middle of something." He looked at Matt. "You're no longer a first timer, you're going to do ten years minimum."

Matt held his face with his hands and looked down at the floor for a long time. Finally, he raised his head. "So you want Tommy?"

"We want you to tell us everything. I want you to tell us about Jay, too."

Matt took a deep breath. Giving up Tommy was one thing, but he and Jay had been friends since they were seven years old. "I can't do that."

"Well you have to get him to help us too or he's going down, Matt, it's just a matter of time."

"I'll talk to him."

Pratt sat back down and leaned forward. "I really want Tommy."

Matt looked at Pratt. The man looked serious. Matt knew that he would get Tommy with or without his help. He wanted to save his own ass but he didn't know if he would want to be known as a rat. He didn't know if he could live with the stigma.

When Tonya entered Summer's home, Summer burst into tears. "I think I'm pregnant."

"What? By who? How did this happen?"

"It's Q's child. I mean, I haven't had sex with Tommy in a while."

"Damn, does he know?" Tonya asked as she embraced her girl.

"No, not yet. I don't know how he's gonna take it."

"What about Tommy?"

"Haven't told him. Haven't spoke to him in a while. He probably hates my guts. I let his girl listen to him say he loved me on a three-way call."

"You did what?" Tonya asked.

"That's a long story, Tonya." Summer paced. "What am I going to do? I don't know nothing about raising a baby. I can't take care of a baby."

"Are you sure that you're pregnant?"

"No, I'm not sure, but I think I am. I took the home pregnancy test and the results came back positive."

"Are you serious?"

"Yeah."

"What? Girl, are you crazy? Why did you have unprotected sex?"

Summer shrugged. "It just happened. I don't know how it happened, it just did."

"Come on, Summer. Having unprotected sex doesn't just happen. You knew he didn't have a condom on."

"So what are you here to do"¦ get in my shit?"

Tonya embraced Summer "No, baby, I am here for you." She then held her face. "But you have to tell Q."

Summer stepped away. "I don't want to."

"What do you think he will say?"

Summer made eye contact with Tonya then turned away. "I don't know what he'll say."

"But you have to tell him."

"I know, and I have to tell Tommy," Summer said.

Tonya stared at Summer. "I don't think you should tell Tommy just yet."

"Why not?"

"Because you don't even know if Q wants the baby or not."

Summer frowned. She hadn't thought about that possibility. She thought that maybe he would be a little upset because of the unexpected pregnancy but she'd never thought that he would want to abort the baby. Summer said, "You know what? I am going to keep the baby regardless of whether he supports me or not."

"You think you can support a baby?"

"Yeah."

"Summer, you braid hair and you're trying to write a book that may or may not sell."

"I can't abort my baby. I will not abort a baby." She turned away. For the first time she was afraid. Tears rolled down her face. She finally looked at Tonya and said, "I don't know what to do."

Tonya hugged her tightly.

33

Summer was lying across her bed when she heard a loud knock. She opened the door; it was Tommy. "Hey, haven't I told you about popping up at my house?"

"Hey, I tried calling you and you didn't answer the damn phone."

"Tommy, can you leave me the hell alone? You have your woman. Could you just leave?"

"Let me come in for a minute."

She reluctantly let him inside. He followed her to the living room. "Summer, what the hell is your problem?"

"My problem, nigga? What do you mean my problem? You are the one with the jealous-ass girlfriend."

"And you expect me to believe that you ain't got nobody?"

She thought about Q. She thought about the baby. She wondered if Tommy knew something. This was the second time he'd showed up at her house unannounced. Maybe he had seen Q leaving her house before. She'd known some guys to be stalkers.

"Why don't you keep it real with me? I know something is going on with you. I know you have somebody else," Tommy said.

"Tommy, you're tripping man."

He began to pace. "Am I tripping? Tell me how am I tripping? You had me telling you that I loved you over the phone."

"So you didn't mean it?"

"Of course I love you."

"So why in the hell did it matter that the bitch heard it?"

He stopped pacing. "Because."

"Because what?" She was now in his face.

"Just because."

"Because you love that bitch too." She said the word with so much venom and hatred Tommy stepped backward.

"I don't understand," he said.

"You don't understand what?"

"What happened"|what happened to us?"

"Tommy, we grew apart that's all." Summer turned her back and folded her arms. "People grow apart you know."

"Yeah, but"|"

"Tommy stop it. You weren't going to tell her about me."

"Yeah eventually."

She turned and faced him again, then looked directly in his eyes. "Tommy, it's run its course." She smiled. "We've had some good times, actually some great times, but it has run its course."

There was a long silence in the room. Finally he said, "I guess so."

At a Starbuck's in the University area, Matt nursed a cup of coffee as he waited on his friend Jay. Jay noticed something was bothering Matt as soon as he approached the table. What's wrong?"

"Nothing."

"Come on man, you can tell me."

"It's over, man. The gig is over."

Jay sat down at the table still confused. "I don't understand."

"I know you don't."

"What the fuck are you talking about, man?"

"Man it's the feds, man. They got me. They picked me up yesterday."

"For what?"

Matt leaned forward. "Those goddamn cars, man."

"Oh, shit, man," Jay said. He stood and ran his fingers through his hair.

"Man, can you just sit your ass down for a minute?"

Jay sat back down. "What are we going to do now?"

"Don't worry, we will be okay."

"How in the hell did you get out?"

Matt took a deep breath. "I agreed to give somebody up."

"What the fuck are you saying, man? Did you rat on me?"

"Now if I ratted on you would I be telling you what's going on?"

"So who did you give up?"

"Nobody."

"I still don't understand."

"They want me to give up Tommy."

"How the hell do they know about Tommy?"

"It's this agent Pratt motherfucker. He knows everything. He knows about you and me. He has pictures."

"Pictures?"

"Yeah."

"So why didn't he want me since he knows about me?"

"Because I saved your ass that's why. I refused to give you up."

"But you're giving up Tommy?"

"I have no choice."

"Damn."

"I know," Matt said, looking at the ceiling. He didn't want to give Tommy up but he didn't know what else to do.

When Tommy stepped outside of the hotel, J-Black approached him. "Fatboy."

"Damn, man. You out of the hospital already?"

"Can't keep a real nigga down."

"What can I help you with?"

J-Black stared him right in the eyes. "Two things""I need some bread and I need to know where that nigga Q lives."

Tommy dug into his pocket and peeled off five $100 bills.

"I need at least five more."

Tommy thought back to when J-Black would rob him. He felt like he was being extorted.

"I can't do it."

"Listen, Tommy. I ain't trying to rough nothing off. I'm just trying to live, you know. I mean, I did just take some hot ones for doing a job for you."

Tommy knew he was right, and he felt kind of bad for J-Black. He gave him five more $100 bills.

"Thanks, man. Now I need to know where that nigga Q lives, man."

"I don't know where he lives."

"Damn." J-Black sounded disappointed, then he remembered the night that he killed those three clowns, they'd showed him where Q's man Country lived. He had all the information he needed.

Q saw the pregnancy test on the sink. The results were positive. A baby, he thought. He damn sure didn't need that shit in his life. He stormed out the bathroom holding the test in his hand. When he entered Summer's bedroom, he found her talking on the cell phone. "Summer, what the fuck is this?" "Tonya let me call you back." She terminated the call.

"So what the hell is going on?"

"I'm pregnant, Q. Hell, you see the test."

"So what are you going to do about it?"

She looked away. Now all of a sudden it was what was she going to do about it. What about him? Hadn't he slept with her?

"Q, I'm having the baby."

"Summer, I ain't ready for no damn baby."

"So what are you saying? Are you saying that you ain't gonna help me?"

"No."

"What are you saying?"

"I ain't ready for no baby."

"And I am?" Summer said, sucking her teeth. "Trust me. I did not try to get pregnant."

"I thought you were on the pill."

"I never said that."

"Why did you make me screw you raw?"

"Make you? Nigga I ain't never make a nigga get no pussy, and I damn sure ain't make you get it; you did have a choice."

Q stared at the pregnancy test again. He couldn't believe it had happened to him again. He had one baby's mother that he didn't get along with, and he knew, though Summer was cool, that if you brought a baby into the picture all of that would change.

"So what you want me to do, Quentin?"

He wanted her to abort the baby, but he couldn't say that. It would be heartless.

"I don't know."

"Me either," she said, looking away.

He sat on the bed still holding the test. He looked up at Summer. "You know I didn't ask for this."

"You see Q, when you say shit like that it makes you seem like the insensitive motherfucker that you are."

"You don't know me."

"I'm realizing that."

"You want me to get an abortion, Q? Why don't you just go ahead and say that you want me to kill the baby; kill your child."

"How do I know it's mine?" I mean, you did have a boyfriend or a sugar daddy when I met you."

"What the fuck are you talking about?"

"Talking about fat-ass Tommy. I know you were fuckin' him too."

"You know Tommy?"

"Yeah," Q said, avoiding her eyes.

"How do you know him?"

He laughed then walked to the other side of the room as he thought of how he would explain it to her that he knew him.

"Quentin, how do you know Tommy?"

"I've known him for a long time. Tommy has sold me cars."

"How did you know that I had been with him?"

"Fuck that shit. Answer my question first. Is it my baby or his baby?"

Summer ran her fingers through her hair. This was too much for her to deal with. Were Q and Tommy playing with her or something? How in the hell did they know each other? Was Q telling her the truth? Did Tommy sell him cars? So many questions; she needed answers.

"So is it mine or Tommy's?"

"You're an asshole."

"You can say what you want, but you ain't trapping Q with no damn baby."

"Nigga it's yours and you're going to pay for it."

"That'll be the day."

Summer walked over and stood so close to Q she could almost taste his breath, then she stepped away. "You know what, Q? Fuck you. I don't need shit from you."

"How many months are you pregnant?"

"I don't know."

"My point exactly. You don't know if it's mine or Tommy's."

"Q, how the fuck do you know Tommy?"

He left the room without answering.

34

I got a Maserati for eighty thousand, Tommy," Matt said.

"Don't talk like that," Tommy said, looking at his phone.

"What you talking about?" Matt said. "Relax, Tommy. It's not like we're drug dealers. We're car thieves. Nobody is watching us."

Tommy relaxed a little. He knew Matt was right, plus he trusted him.

"What color is the car?"

"Silver. Tommy, you're going to love it."

"Eighty huh?"

"Hell yeah. Man, this is a steal."

"I can't make no money off this car, man. If you charge me eighty how in the hell am I going to make some money? I will have to sell it for one hundred."

Mark Pratt wrote down 60K on the yellow piece of paper. "Sixty thousand and it's yours," Matt said.

Tommy's mind went back to Q. He knew he was stupid enough to take the car. But they weren't friends anymore. He thought about Dino, a big player from Atlanta he'd done fed time with. He'd ran into him a few months ago. Dino was driving a Maybach. "Okay, can you wait until Thursday? I have some things to take care of."

Matt looked at agent Pratt who was shaking his head no.

"I can't, man. We have to do it today."

"I can't do it today. I have to take care of some things. Right now I'm living in a hotel. I gotta find me a place to stay."

Pratt scribbled on the paper, Thursday is fine.

"I will see if I can hold it till Thursday."

FBI agent Connors said, "We have enough to indict him."

Country was about to get into his Chevy Tahoe when a man walked up behind him then put a gun against his back and said, "Walk with me."

"What the fuck is going on?"

"I got a 9mm on your back, and if you make one move I swear I'll . . ."

"Who are you?"

"Motherfucker walk back into your house!"

Country attempted to look at the man.

"Don't try nothing. I will blow your back out!"

"What the fuck is going on?"

"Back in your house."

When they were back in the house the man made Country take a seat on the sofa. He sat across from him in a recliner. Country didn't recognize the man; never saw him in his life. "What are you here for?"

Smiling, the man said, "Revenge. You niggas didn't think you were going to try to kill me and get away with it did you?"

"What the fuck are you talking about?"

"Nigga, I'm the motherfucker that you tried to kill."

"I ain't try to kill nobody," Country said.

"Where the fuck is Q?"

"Q?" Country said, trying to sound puzzled.

The man was now in Country's face. "In case you haven't realized it, I'm J-Black, the nigga that you tried to kill."

"I'm telling you, man, I ain't have nothing to do with that."

J-Black grimaced. "Call Q. Call that motherfucker now."

"That's my brother," Country said, realizing that J-Black

was the nigga that killed Puff and "~em. He knew that if he called Q they would both end up dead.

"That's my brother," he repeated.

"I don't give a fuck who he is. Call him or you going to hell tonight." He put the gun against Country's face. The steel was cold against his temple. Country struck J-Black's arm, causing him to fall backward, but J-Black still held onto the gun.

Country charged J-Black, grabbed him and then buried his fingernails into his neck.

J-Black pumped three shots into Country's chest. His body crashed to the ground face first.

> Dear Summer,
>
> I thought you were a cool chick, I mean, everything started out so good, but now you trying to trap a nigga off like that. That is not how you do a real nigga. I mean I was digging you and all, and who knows where the relationship would have gone, but now I can't see nothing good coming out of this situation. I mean, if you decide to have the baby, I'm telling you right now, you ain't getting no support from me, even if it's mine.
>
> Q

Summer showed her Blackberry screen to Tonya.

"Can you believe this nigga?"

"Damn," Tonya said. She handed the phone back to her.

Summer sat on the sofa. A single tear rolled down her face. She wiped her face with her T-shirt. "I don't know what to do."

"You going to have the baby, that's what you're going to do."

"Hell no. I mean, I want to, I really wanted to, not because I want his child but because I really wanted something. I feel lonely sometimes, you know?"

Tonya held her friend. She was shivering, not because it was cold, it was more of a nervous shiver. Why was Q acting so nasty? Why didn't he believe the baby was his?

Summer wiped her face again then pulled away from Tonya. "I forgot to tell you"¦"

"Tell me what?"

"Q knows Tommy, and he knows that I used to fuck him."

"Are you serious?"

"How does he know this?"

"I don't know. Maybe he asked somebody. Hell, I have no idea."

"You didn't ask him?"

"Yeah, of course I did," Summer said, her mind drifting to Tommy, wondering how he was going to react once he found out that she was pregnant. But not only was she pregnant, but pregnant by somebody else"¦"pregnant by somebody that knew him.

"What did he say?"

"I think he may have bought cars from Tommy, I don't know how he knew that me and Tommy had been together."

"Charlotte is small. Maybe he heard it in the street or something."

Summer raised her shirt and looked down at her belly. "If it's a girl I'ma name her Aaliya."

"I think you're gonna have a boy."

"Don't say that."

"Why not? My sister has boys and she says boys are easy."

She thought about the possibility of having a boy. How would she raise him alone? She had heard that boys were a handful. They wanted to play sports, were very mischievous, and broke things. She didn't know if she was prepared for that.

"So you're certain you're going to go through with it?"

Summer looked Tonya in her eyes, fearful about the future. "Yeah I want to go through with it"¦I think."

"You think?"

Summer covered her face again. "I don't know." The tears came again, and when she finally composed herself she said, "I don't know. Maybe I will have an abortion."

When Q saw Country's mom's phone number come across his screen, he answered immediately. "Hello, Ms. Anne."

"My baby is dead, Quentin. My baby is gone."

"Calm down, Ms. Anne. What are you talking about?"

"Country was found dead last night. He was shot three times in the chest."

Q's heart dropped. His mouth was dry. Was this some kind of dream? He looked at his phone again and the caller ID indicated that it was Country's mom alright.

"What happened?"

"I don't know, baby. I was calling you to see if you knew anything," she said, still sobbing. He heard Country's sisters Shakira and Shante in the background crying.

"Ms. Anne, I don't know what happened, but I promise you I will get to the bottom of this shit." He checked his watch; it was 3:00 p.m. He knew something was strange. He hadn't talked to Country since yesterday.

"Baby don't get yourself in no trouble. You have to let the Lord handle this."

"But Ms. Anne, my brother" your son is gone."

"And Quentin, there ain't nothing neither one of us can do to bring him back. Remember that."

"Okay, bye Ms. Anne." He terminated the call. Who the fuck could have killed Country and why?

Tommy and Angie met at the Flying Biscuit, a trendy little restaurant in Ballantyne. She didn't really want to meet with him, but he had begged, and she agreed to hear what he had to say. They both ordered shrimp and grits.

There was an awkward silence before Tommy asked, "So where do we go from here, Angie?"

"What do you mean?" she said, stirring her grits.

"I mean is it over?"

"As far as I'm concerned."

"Look me in my eyes and tell me it's over," he said.

She stared him right in his eyes. "It's over Tommy."

"What about the baby?"

"Tommy, I'm not pregnant."

"Really? How do you know?"

"I went to see my doctor."

His expression turned to disappointment. He grabbed a shrimp and shoved it into his mouth.

"I see you've been practicing your table manners."

"I'm disappointed," he said, ignoring her sarcasm.

"Why?"

"You know how bad I want kids," he said as he held another shrimp in his hand. "I really want a son."

"But we're not ready."

"I think we are."

She laughed, and he became annoyed. She knew how sensitive he was about this subject; she knew just what it took to make him mad.

The waitress refilled their glasses with lemonade.

"Don't laugh."

"But the relationship is a joke," she said. Her eyes were misty again.

"It's a joke to you."

"It was apparently a joke to you."

He leaned forward, but without looking into her eyes, he said, "What happened to us?"

"She happened to us. Your little girlfriend."

"She's not my girlfriend."

"But you love her don't you?"

He didn't respond.

"Yeah, of course you love her." She took a bite of her food.

The waitress dropped the check on the table.

"Where are you living now?" he asked, changing the subject.

"Mama's house. Where else? I mean, I can't go back to my house. I almost got killed."

"Nobody's going to kill you."

"You don't know that."

"Trust me," he said, and then gulped down his lemonade.

"They tried already."

"They were gunning for me."

"You weren't there. You left me."

"I left you because you made me leave."

Silence. Neither one of them had anything to say. Finally he grabbed her hand. "You still love me don't you?"

Tears rolled down her face, and he stood to pull his chair to the same side of the table she was on. She pulled a Kleenex from her purse and wiped her face. She didn't respond to his question. She turned to him and buried her head into his chest. He brushed her hair playfully then whispered, "Let's get out of here. I want you to spend the night with me."

He picked up the check, $22.99, and then pulled three tens from his wallet before they left.

35

Someone was flashing his or her headlights behind him. Tommy looked in the rearview mirror. He recognized the car immediately. It was Q. What the hell did he want? Did he have someone with him? Tommy looked under his armrest. He didn't have his gun. He pulled over at a gas station two miles later. He knew it would be safe there to see what Q wanted. Both men got out of their vehicles and stood face to face. "What's up Q?"

"You know damn well what's up. Country is dead."

"What the fuck you mean?"

"He dead" like somebody licked him. What part of dead don't you understand?"

"When did this happen? How did this happen?"

"He was shot in the chest," Q said, examining Tommy's body language. He believed Tommy had something to do with it, but he didn't look or act as if he were guilty of anything, but he never did. That was a quality he had. Now Q was sure he had something to do with Squirt getting arrested like he was sure he had something to do with Country's death.

Tommy placed his hands on Q's shoulders and said, "Look at me man, I ain't have shit to do with this. I swear to you I didn't."

"Motherfucker, Country was like my brother. You know how close we were."

"I didn't have nothing to do with it."

"Why'd you do it Tommy?"

Ignoring his question, Tommy asked, "Did you have J-Black shot?"

"So he did it?" Q asked.

"Could have," Tommy said, then looked away. His truck was running. He reached in the truck and turned off the ignition. He walked over to put his arm around Q. "I didn't know Country was dead."

"That was my brother, man." He balled his fist up as if he wanted to punch Tommy, but he began to pace and think. The 9mm was in the car under the seat. He could just shoot Tommy in the head and drive off, but those damn surveillance cameras were located above the gas pumps.

"I understand, and trust me, I hate that this shit has happened. It has to stop."

"Can't stop now," Q said.

"Why not"|why can't it stop? Do you want everybody to die? Is that how you want this shit to end?"

"Nigga I don't give a fuck. I stopped giving a fuck today. I swear to you, Tommy, somebody is going to pay for this"|you're going to pay for this."

Q jerked away from Tommy and headed back to his car. When he got in the car he pulled up beside Tommy and said, "Watch your back, nigga."

Summer looked down at her stomach. It looked as if she were bloated. There was a pudge. She knew that she was going to look funny pregnant. She was small and she probably wouldn't remain small throughout her pregnancy. Her mother was small; it was in her genes. Rubbing her belly she couldn't believe a baby was inside of her. A living breathing person was inside her.

She was actually going to be a mom. Smiling, she was happy that she was going to make her mother and father grandparents. She didn't care if Q wanted the baby or not. She would take care of her child herself.

She heard a knock at the door. She opened the blinds slightly. Tommy's Range Rover. What the hell did he want? She wouldn't open the door. He might have wanted her to have sex. She couldn't have sex with him. She wouldn't have sex with him. She didn't want him to see her pudge. She didn't open the door. He called. She didn't answer the phone. He sent her a message.

> Dear Summer,
>
> I just left your house. Your car was in the driveway, so I am assuming that you are sleeping or you just don't want to be bothered. Either way, I am fine. I really need to talk to you about some things. I had a heart to heart talk with Angie, and I think that I am going to try to do right by her. I mean, I still love you and all, but I have a gut feeling that you're becoming serious with somebody else. I feel like we've grown apart.
> Tommy
> Sent via Sprint PCS Blackberry

"We have to get this nigga, man," Ditty said while reclining the seat back in Tommy's truck. He lit a blunt, inhaled, then blew out a ring of smoke and then coughed. "Yeah, this shit is getting serious."

"The shit is already serious," Tommy said. He rolled the window down, trying not to inhale the smoke. Usually he didn't allow anyone to smoke in his truck, but now he really could care less. He was thinking about the conversation he'd had with Q.

"I don't give a fuck about Q, man. I been telling you all along let's get that nigga, man. I'm telling you, he's a pussy. I mean, I can see it in him. Now that Country is dead, he really don't have nobody to ride with him."

"This shit is really fucked up, man. I mean, all this shit came about because these niggas think I ratted."

Ditty coughed again before putting the blunt out in the ashtray. "I don't give a fuck how it came about. Now it's about to be war, man. We gotta get him before he get at one of us."

"I ain't afraid to die," Tommy said.

"It ain't about being afraid. I ain't afraid either, but I don't want to die now, and I don't believe you do either."

Tommy didn't say anything. He thought about the bridge.

"So do we get him?" Ditty asked.

"We have to protect ourselves."

"Naw, nigga. We have to take him out."

Tommy looked at Ditty, not really knowing what to say. He knew Ditty was right.

It was three in the morning when Tommy's phone rang. It was a number he wasn't familiar with. He answered it on the third ring. Maybe somebody was in trouble. "Hello."

"Tommy, it's Jay."

"Jay, it's three in the morning, what's wrong?"

"I have to talk to you and it can't wait."

"What's wrong?"

"I'd rather see you in person. Can we meet at IHOP on Independence? The one going to Interstate 485."

"When?"

"Now, Tommy. I really need to see you."

"Where's Matt?"

"He won't be with me."

"Why not?"

"Tommy, just come see me."

"Is Matt in trouble?"

"Meet me at IHOP in one hour."

3 6

Jay was at a table in the back of the restaurant nursing a glass of orange juice when Tommy came in and sat across from him. Jay looked nervous—bags had formed beneath his eyes. Tommy could tell that he hadn't rested well. "What's wrong?"

Jay leaned forward and avoided Tommy's eyes, but he didn't say anything. He grabbed his glass and placed it to his lips. He was killing time.

"Jay, tell me what's wrong?"

He looked Tommy directly in the eyes. "Tommy, don't show up to get the Maserati."

"What the hell are you talking about?"

"Tommy, the feds got Matt."

"I just spoke with Matt."

"I know, and he was with the feds. Your whole conversation was recorded."

Tommy felt queasy. He was at a loss for words. "Why Jay¦ why did Matt do me like this?"

"They know about all the cars he's sold. They had him, and it came down to between you and him, Tommy. I'm sorry."

Tommy laughed. He got it. Now it had to be a joke. "You're kidding me, right? This is a joke, right, Jay?"

Jay's eyes looked serious. "Tommy, I wouldn't wake you up in the middle of the night to play with you."

"I gotta take him out. I cannot go back to prison, man. I can't."

"Tommy, didn't you hear me? Matt is working for the feds. You don't want to do nothing to him."

Tommy stood and frisked Jay. "What about you?"

"What about me?"

"Are you in trouble too?"

"No. He spared me."

"What the fuck? Why in the hell did he do this to me?"

Jay looked away from Tommy. He was in deep thought. "Tommy, it just ain't right, man."

Tommy slammed his fist hard on the table. "Damn it! I've been pinched again."

"They got you, Tommy."

"All they got is conversation."

"That's enough to go to the grand jury."

"I gotta get outta here."

"You can't let them know that you know, or else they are going to get you."

"I got to get rid of my phone."

Jay looked puzzled. "Why?"

"These damn things have GPS on them. They can track my movements," Tommy said, wondering where he would run.

"You need your phone, Tommy. This is how you can keep your enemies close. You can kind of gauge their movements."

"You're right." Tommy looked Jay in his eyes. They were blue eyes. White man eyes, but they were sincere eyes. He asked Jay, "Why are you helping me?"

He took a deep breath. "You seem to be a good person."

"But I'm a crook, and you're a crook."

"But we're the good guys, Tommy. We have loyalty."

Both men stood, knowing this would be the last time Tommy would see Jay. He hugged him and whispered, "Thanks a lot."

By the time J.C. realized that the intruders were in his house, the two men with ski masks were standing right over his bed. "Get the hell out of here!"

"Shut the fuck up, old man," the short one said.

"I don't have no money."

The short one stuffed the gun into J.C.'s mouth, breaking his new veneers. J.C. tried to stand up from the bed, but his efforts were useless. Shorty let off five shots, killing J.C. instantly.

When Tommy's phone rang, the number came up private. He answered. It was J-Black.

"I need some bread, man."

"I don't have no dough," Tommy said, remembering he would need all his money for running. He had to save what little bit he had left.

"Listen, man, I just need a couple of hundred dollars, nothing major."

"Okay, I can probably swing that. Can you meet me in front of my hotel in about an hour?"

"I'm not far. I can be there in fifteen minutes."

J-Black was sitting on top of the Magnum when Tommy came out. Tommy gave him the two $100 bills and asked, "Did you kill Country?"

J-Black folded the money and put it into his front pocket. "Some things you are better off not knowing, Tommy. You know that. You've been in the game long enough."

"Why?"

"Because the niggas tried to kill me," J-Black said. He lifted his shirt to show Tommy the staples where he had been shot. They crossed the center of his stomach and made a lowercase t.

"Damn."

"Damn is right." He stared at Tommy with serious eyes. "And as soon as I find that faggot-ass Q, it's over for him too."

"I think you should chill. You've killed four people already."

"Besides Q, you and Scooter are the only people that knows."

"Your point?"

"Nigga, keep your fuckin' mouth shut and I'll be alright," J-Black said as he lit a Newport.

"Don't worry about me. I'm on your side."

The smoke came from J-Black's nostrils. "Well, if you're on my side, help me out."

"I don't understand."

"I need some money, man."

"I can't help you with that."

"I'm not trying to extort you or nothing, but bro' I really need some paper. If you can't help me, put me on a lick or something."

Tommy thought for a moment then said, "I really don't have anything for you to do."

J-Black pulled his gun from his back pocket and moved it to his waist. "I need another $200."

Tommy pulled two more hundred dollar bills from his wallet and passed them off.

37

Tommy was surprised when he saw Angie through the peephole of his hotel room. He opened the door and she hugged him.

He smiled and looked down at her. "What did I do to deserve this?"

"Tommy, I just realized how much I missed you."

He closed the door and she sat on the bed. The room fell silent and he turned the TV on. She asked him to turn it off. "Let's talk for a minute."

"What you want to talk about?"

"Us."

He paced and then he peered out the hotel room window and wondered if the feds were watching. Where the hell was Mark Pratt? "What about us?"

"Tommy, why won't you do what you're supposed to do?"

He sighed. He had no explanation why he did the things he did. He oftentimes wondered why he had been such a womanizer. Why did counting illegal money give him such a thrill? He had lived most of his life on the edge, but that's who he was and he'd long realized that no penitentiary or counselor could change him.

"I am who I am."

"I know, and I love you."

"But?"

"But, Tommy, I want so much more for us."

"Like what?"

She stood and smiled brightly. "I want a wedding. Not just any old wedding, I want a big wedding in Jamaica with all of my friends and family. I don't want no justice of the peace shit."

"Weddings are just a ceremony. What matters is you love me and I love you"¦" He looked out the curtains again.

"Tommy, what are you looking for?"

"Nothing." He closed the curtain and sat down on the chair beside the window to finish what he was saying. "Let's just go downtown and get it over with, you know, City Hall. Nothing spectacular, but we can go to the Maldive Islands for our honeymoon."

"I want a wedding."

He huffed but didn't respond.

"So where do we go with this roller coaster of a relationship?"

"Where do you want to go?"

"I want it to be me and you without Summer."

"Summer is the past," he said, knowing that Summer had been seeing somebody else.

Their eyes locked. "Is she really the past?"

Tommy moved closer to Angie and ran his fingers through her hair. He touched her butt and she pushed his hand away.

"What's wrong?"

"Tommy, I want to talk."

"Okay I'm listening."

"How do we go again? I mean, I don't know if I can trust you, but I love you."

"Listen, I made some mistakes, but I really love you."

"So can you promise that you won't leave me?"

Tommy wanted to promise her that. He wanted things to go back to what they were before, but he knew that it was just a matter of time before he was brought up on that bullshit indictment. He'd be back in jail, just like Angie was afraid of. She had been right. It was his associates that had brought him down again.

"Promise me, Tommy."

He looked her directly in her eyes. "I will never leave you if I can help it."

She kissed him passionately then pushed him back on the bed and removed her blouse.

Matt called Tommy at 10:00 a.m.

"Hey, Matt. What's up?"

"Wondering what you're going to do?"

"Yeah, yeah," Tommy said, trying not to further incriminate himself just in case he couldn't get away.

"Tommy, we need to do this fast."

"What do we need to do fast?"

"I have the Maserati that you wanted" remember?"

"Can we meet somewhere?" Tommy asked.

"Yeah, where do you want to meet?"

"We can meet at Carolina Place Mall."

"Okay, Tommy. Have the cash with you."

"We can talk business in person."

"Tommy, have the money. I have people calling me for the car every day. I need for you to take it or else I have to sell it to somebody else."

"I'll meet you at two."

"Tommy have the money."

Tommy hung up the phone.

The text message from Summer read, Come over right away.

Tommy got into his truck, and fifteen minutes later he was on her doorstep. She invited him in. Before he could take his seat on the sofa, she said, "Tommy, I'm pregnant."

His jaw dropped in surprise but he didn't say anything.

"Tommy, say something."

"What do you want me to say?"

"I don't know, say anything."

He finally sat down then looked at her, but still he did not respond.

"Don't you want to know when it happened? Who is the baby's daddy?"

"Do you want to tell me? Hell, I'm still shocked. Then again, nothing surprises me with bitches."

"Tommy, why you gotta be disrespectful?"

"Disrespectful? You're the one that's pregnant."

She paced. "So, Tommy, what the hell was I supposed to do? I mean, you have your life with Angie; I was just some ass on the side."

"Ass on the side for me or the nigga that knocked you up?"

"Oh that was a low blow."

Tommy stood. He was about to leave, but she approached him and placed her arms around him. "Don't go, Tommy, please don't go."

He pushed her arms away.

"Baby, can we talk?" she said.

He stared at her coldly. "Talk about what? I mean, the damage is done." He stared at her stomach. She indeed had a pouch.

"Damage?"

"Yeah, damage. I hope you don't think there's a chance for us."

"Nigga, you have a family. That's just it. I never thought there was a chance for us."

"Obviously," he said, then walked toward the door and suddenly stopped. It was all coming back to him. This is why she didn't want him just showing up at her place. She'd had a man the whole time. "Who is he?"

She looked at him, not knowing what to say. She knew that Q knew him, but she didn't know how well they knew each other. She finally said, "A guy named Quentin."

"Quentin? Where the hell does he live?"

"They call him Q."

"Q? A tall dark-skinned nigga; deals dope on the west side?"

"I don't know what he does."

"Yeah, he's a drug dealer."

"How well do you know him?"

"I know the nigga very well. Been at odds with his ass for the past few months, now you wanna go and have this nigga's baby?"

"Tommy, I didn't know."

"Where did you meet him at?"

"Downtown."

"You met him downtown, huh? Where at?"

"I don't remember. I think it was a bar."

Tommy began to pace. "I can't believe this shit. You're about to have a baby by a motherfucker that I can't stand."

"Tommy, I'm sorry."

"How did it happen?"

She ran her fingers through her hair and tried to gather her thoughts. She sat on the sofa.

"Okay, you want to tell me how the fuck did this happen?" he said.

"Tommy, I don't know. We met, he was charming, I was lonely, and he told me some shit that I wanted to hear."

"Remember when I took you to the park a while back?"

"Yeah."

"Remember those niggas?"

"Vaguely."

"Well, one of those niggas was Q. Actually, you may have known that."

"No I met him after the park."

"But you saw him at the park right?"

"Tommy, honestly, I don't remember nobody at the park that day."

"Well maybe he saw you."

"Maybe. I can't speak for him."

"So you keeping the baby?"

"Of course. Why?"

"That's really fucked up."

"Nigga you want me to have an abortion? I can't believe you want me to kill my baby."

Tommy didn't respond. He didn't mean to imply that she should have an abortion.

"So you want me to kill my baby?" She was now in his face.

"Get away from me," he said.

"Tommy what the fuck is going on?"

"The nigga used you. Q used you to get to me."

"What?"

"Yeah, he saw you with me and decided to get back at me by getting with you."

"This isn't making sense."

"One of his friends got busted."

"What the hell does that have to do with me?"

"He thinks I'm the reason he got busted."

"He thinks that you snitched?"

"Yeah, but I didn't. I just sold the nigga the car that he got busted in."

"Oh okay." She paced and thought. She felt used. Was she part of some game that Q and Tommy were playing? Did Q really care anything about her? She turned and faced Tommy. She was now crying. "Tommy, I didn't know that he was one of the guys in the park that day."

"I know, but he knew who you were."

"So what do I do?"

"Do whatever you feel is right."

"No, Tommy. I don't know if I want his baby."

He walked over to her and hugged her. "Do whatever you feel is right."

38

The next morning Tommy headed to J.C's house. When he pulled into the neighborhood, he saw a group of school kids waiting on the bus. One of the kids was off to the side by himself listening to his Ipod. As Tommy drove past the kids he made eye contact with one of them. Tommy recognized him immediately, Danny, the white kid that had sold Q the Ipods. Damn, he was just a kid. Though he looked grown, he was just a kid. Did Q know he was a kid? Did he give a damn?

At that moment Tommy was glad he wasn't a drug-dealer. Selling stolen cars never hurt anybody. That was the way he chose to justify his criminal activity, but when he sold drugs, his mindset was""If the users didn't get it from him they would get it from somebody else.

When he stepped inside his dad's house, he climbed into the attic and got his money. When he came back downstairs, he yelled out to his father, but nobody answered. He continued to yell. He figured that J.C. might have still been asleep, though he was usually up at that time of morning. When he walked into his dad's room, he dropped his bag of money on the floor. The hole in the middle of his father's head and the blood that was splattered on the sheets almost made him vomit. He picked his dad up from the bed and held him for a long time while running his fingers through his hair. He didn't want to believe this. He couldn't believe it. His heart ached for the man who had raised him. He knew that he would never be the same. He continued to brush through his hair with his fingers. He kissed his pops on the jaw and then called the police.

Tommy and Ditty sat on the hood of Ditty's car, which was parked in his driveway. "Yeah, I know Q had something to do with J.C.'s death," Tommy said.

"So how you want to handle it?" Ditty said, revealing his gun.

"I gotta get out of here, Ditty. Shit's about to hit the fan for me."

"What you talking about?"

"Matt did me wrong."

"What you talking about?" Ditty asked, looking confused. "Does he owe you money or something?"

"No."

"I don't understand."

"He set me up."

"If he set you up why are you still here?"

"He got me to talk about buying cars and he was with the feds."

Ditty was silent and tried to make sense out of the whole situation.

"Yeah, they recorded the whole thing."

"How do you know this?"

"Jay told me."

"Damn. Can't trust white boys, can't trust niggas, can't trust drug dealers, and you can't trust car thieves""it's a dirty game and a dirty lifestyle."

"And Summer's pregnant."

"That's a good thing."

"No that's a bad thing. She's pregnant by Q."

"What?!" Ditty said surprised. He pulled out his cigarettes and lit one.

"Yeah, I think he got at her to get back at me."

Ditty gritted his teeth. "Tommy, we got to get this motherfucker. We can't go on like this shit didn't happen."

"I gotta think about myself, Ditty."

"So what's next, Tommy? What's next? What are we going to do?"

Tommy pulled thirty $100 bills from his wallet and handed them to Ditty, along with an address in South Carolina. "I want you to pay to have my pops cremated, and scatter the ashes on the lot on this address."

"Where are you going?"

"Don't ask questions. You will hear from me soon."

Ditty looked at the paper then back at Tommy. He hugged his friend then said, "Take care of yourself."

When Tommy opened the door J-Black stood before him unshaven and dirty. He looked as if he'd been up all night. "Can I come in?"

"What do you want?"

"I just wanna talk," J-Black said.

Tommy pulled his gun from his back pocket and cocked it. He was not going to go out being stupid. J-Black could not be trusted.

J-Black smiled. "Man, you can put the gun up. There ain't gonna be no problems."

"I don't trust you, nigga."

J-Black eased into the room and walked to the other side. He sat at a table by the window and peered out. "Have you ever wondered what you're going to do next? I mean, where your next meal is going to come from?"

"What the fuck are you getting at?"

J-Black looked at Tommy. "I need money, and I need help."

"You always need money."

"Yeah, but I need help, man. I mean, I'm 34-years-old and I've run these streets for the longest man, coming up on big licks. Do you know I robbed a dope dealer for 38 kilos last summer?"

"It's a wonder you're not dead."

"I know. I've did a lot of shit, Tommy, and I'm tired."

"I know the feeling."

"Right now I don't give a fuck if the cops know if I killed Country. In fact, I think they know."

"How do you know?"

"Somebody said they flashed my picture across the six o'clock news."

"Really?"

"Yeah, I think so, I don't give a fuck."

Tommy sat on the bed. Never really knowing this side of J-Black, he actually felt kind of sorry for him.

"Can you give me a thousand dollars?"

"What you going to do with it?"

"Get high, fuck a bitch"¦I don't know, man."

Tommy knew J-Black was an addict, but this was the first time he had ever discussed it with him. The man had robbed so many people in the past, but he could never manage to keep any money.

"So can you help me?"

"I don't have any money."

"Come on, man, help me. I need to smoke."

"I don't have no money."

J-Black's eyes grew; his lips were dry. "Tommy, I need to smoke. I need a job. I'll do anything for you. Just give me some money, man."

Tommy walked over to J-Black and grabbed him by the arm. "Come on, man, you gotta get the fuck out of here."

J-Black said, "Listen, man, I'm sorry. I need some money"¦ I'll do anything you want me to do. Do you have a job for me? I'll kill whoever you need me to kill."

Tommy thought long and hard before saying, "Hey I got an idea."

39

Q opened the door at Summer's home. Tommy aimed the gun right at his head. He had gone to Summer's place after leaving J-Black. "Nigga step inside."

Summer walked into the room and saw what was going on. She screamed. "Tommy! Put the gun down!"

"Shut the fuck up!"

Q held his hands up. "Nigga you ain't gonna kill me. You ain't got the heart to kill nobody."

Tommy fired the gun. The bullet hit Q in the leg and he fell to the floor.

"Motherfucker, did you think you would live to see your child?" Q's eyes grew as he stared down the barrel of the gun. "Come on, Tommy. Let's talk."

"Talk? Now you want to talk?" Tommy slapped him with the gun. "Before I was a snitch; a few minutes ago I didn't have the heart to kill yo punk ass."

"Tommy please don't kill him," Summer said.

He turned and faced her.

"Don't want me to kill your baby's daddy, huh?"

"I don't want you to get in trouble. I could care less about this nigga."

Tommy yanked her by the arm. "Get over there where he is."

"So, nigga, did you think you would kill my pops and get away with it?"

"I didn't kill yo pops."

Tommy fired another shot, hitting him in the shoulder.

"Oh God! God the bullets are so hot. I need water."

"Water? You don't need no water, you're going to be dead in a minute."

"Tommy please think about your life. You're too young to be in jail the rest of your life."

"Summer, you know I wanted a baby."

"I know you did and you still can Tommy, you're only 32."

"Summer, how can you have this motherfucker's baby?"

"Tommy, I'm sorry. I didn't know that he knew you."

Tommy placed the gun up to Q's temple. "Did you think you could play me and get away with it?"

"No."

"I think you thought you could play me" thought that I wasn't going to find out, huh?"

"No, I swear to you it didn't happen the way you think."

"I'm a snitch, right?"

"I don't know," Q said, "All I know is what Squirt told me."

"Your boy told you I snitched on him."

"I need water, please, let me get some water" I think I'm going to die."

"You are going to die. I'm going to blow your fuckin' brains out."

Summer grabbed Tommy's arm. "Please! Please, Tommy, don't do it!"

"You killed my pops."

"No I didn't. Really I didn't," Q said. Sweat poured down his face.

"And fucked my lady; got her pregnant."

"I didn't know she was your lady."

Tommy fired the gun. Q's head exploded like a watermelon on pavement.

Summer screamed, "Oh my God, Tommy! Have you lost your fuckin' mind!?"

He put the gun up to her head.

"No, Tommy!"

"Do you know how much you hurt me?"

"Please, Tommy. Please don't do it."

"I gotta do this, you don't understand."

"Tommy, I have a baby on the way."

"I know, but it's not my baby."

She grabbed his arm. "Tommy, give me the gun."

He held it tightly.

"You don't want to kill me."

"I don't want to kill you, but I'm hurt."

"Let go of the gun."

He released it. She put her arms around his waist and held him.

When J-Black arrived in the mall parking lot, he looked around for the man he was supposed to meet. Tommy said he would be driving a Ford F150. After circling the parking lot for five minutes J-Black spotted the car, so he parked in front of the mall in the space right next to the handicapped space, just like Tommy told him. The white man parked the F150 and walked over to J-Black's vehicle. J-Black popped the lock and the man got into the car.

"Who the fuck are you?" Matt asked.

J-Black pulled the gun from his waist. "Give me the fuckin' money."

"I ain't got no money."

J-Black pumped two shots into Matt's chest.

ATF, DEA, and FBI agents came from nowhere.

"Oh shit," J-Black said as he attempted to raise his gun.

Forty-seven rounds of shots were let off into J-Black's vehicle. He died at the scene.

John Bailey thought it was just another day at the river, until he saw a man's hat and cell phone, and a ring on the bank. He put his pole down and walked around the river with his dog Oscar to see if he could find the person the items belonged to. He didn't, and Oscar, his faithful hound dog, didn't pick up a human scent, so he fished "'til about noon, occasionally wondering where the person was who'd left the items. Several hours later he was leaving the river and he saw a black SUV parked on the side of the bridge. He pulled his old pickup beside the SUV thinking maybe the owner also owned the items. He opened the unlocked door and found a note lying on the seat.

> To Whoever finds this note,
> Life was hard and never fair, I have lived 32 years in this world and the world was never fair to a real black man. The so called American Dream has always been unattainable to most of the people who come from where I come from. See I came from the bottom of the bottom of the barrel. I don't want to come off as bitter, but more of a man that states facts. In my life I had a little fun, had some blessings, but I have always been running and chasing that dream, that unattainable dream. Dealt a little drugs" not because I wanted to, but because I had to. Some might say you didn't have to deal drugs, but I think I had to. I had to be a criminal to get the things that I felt I deserved. I mean, why should my life be dormant when billionaires are taking shuttles to Mars for the hell of it? My mother died when I was young, and I was raised by my stepfather who was later accused of rape by a white woman. He served time and was later found innocent of the crime; happens every day. A black man looks like a criminal because he's a black man. My stepfather was killed a few days ago. Now that he's gone and me being with no kids I have nothing to live for. My only request is that whoever finds this letter call Angie at 704-555-0009 and tell her I love her.
> Tommy

Dear Summer,

I have always loved you. Okay, I had another woman, but hey, what man don't? The point I'm trying to make is that we could have had something special. I think we had something special, but now all of that is over. You had no self control. You had to go out and fuck somebody, huh? You just had to do it. And to make matters worse, you fucked the nigga that I couldn't stand. Somebody that wanted me dead. The man that killed my father. There's a lot you didn't know about me and Q's history, or maybe you did and you just didn't give a fuck. But really, I didn't want it to come down to this, but put yourself in my shoes. A motherfucker talking shit about me saying that I'm a snitch, something that I have never been. And to make matters worse, the nigga killed my stepfather. The only man I have ever loved. Summer, I would have bet my last dollar to anyone that you would have been loyal to me, but you weren't. I don't know why I love you, Summer. You hurt me so bad.

Tommy

Dear Summer,

You don't know me, my name is Jerome but they call me Squirt. Q's friend. He told me to write you if I had something to tell him. Well I do. I need you to tell Q that Tommy had nothing to do with me getting busted. I got my discovery motion back today and it seems as if my dumb ass baby's mama forgot to register my tag. Tell him to apologize to Tommy for me and also tell him that I need some money on my books; maybe a hundred dollars should hold me.

Squirt

Summer read the letter over again. From what she could gather, Q thought Tommy had snitched on his friend, so he tried to kill him, but Tommy wasn't nobody's punk. He went to war against Q and his people. People died, a love triangle spurned, and a baby was on the way. What a perfect book. She at least had something to write about, and she had to write it. She didn't have a baby's father and didn't have a job. She thought it was depressing how things had turned out. She rubbed her belly and thought of her child as a blessing.

Angie was at work when she received a call from a private number. She answered it.

"Hello."

"Hey, baby."

"The news said you were dead."

"I know, but I'm not."

"Thank God," she said. She was elated. He could hear it in her voice.

"Come outside."

She grabbed her coat and went outside. Tommy was in a green Ford Explorer. She got in the truck smiling. She hugged him. "I'm so happy you're here."

He kissed her lips.

"I've got some good news."

"What?"

"I'm pregnant."

He took a deep breath then hugged her tight. "I'm so damn happy," he said. He knew he would have to live life as if he were dead because if the police found out, he would have to be on the run"⸌but it was better than being dead.